MW00454035

Call It Even

EDWIN MARKHAM

Copyright © 2016 Edwin Markham

All rights reserved.

ISBN: 9781549897634

DEDICATION

To my wife, Dorryann, whose support and encouragement
made this possible.

CONTENTS

ACKNOWLEDGMENTS

I would like to thank my son, Dennis, for his many helpful comments over several drafts of this work. He gave me encouragement when I deserved it and brutally honest criticism when I needed it. I would also like to thank author Jessica Speart and her class at Westport Writers' Workshop, for the same reasons.

CHAPTER 1

He waited just beyond the back yard, hidden by the dark, for the lights inside to go out. There were houses on either side, but they were dark and showed no signs of life. This was on the edge of town, and there was nothing behind him but open desert. From watching over several nights, he'd learned that the man of the house came home before the lights went out, or didn't come home until the next morning. The first few times he'd come merely to watch and learn. After that he'd always come prepared, but on previous nights the man had come home before lights out. Not this time.

That big German Shepherd would've been a problem. It had nearly given him away the first night, but the man had restrained it, probably assuming that it was barking at a coyote or a jack rabbit. The man had called it Major. The next night, he'd brought a bowl of anti-freeze for Major, and he hadn't seen him since. 'Acute kidney failure,' he thought, smiling, it works every time. They probably suspected one of their neighbors. Mother said dogs were unclean.

The fact that the dog was an officer, a Major no less, had been a bonus. He hated officers. If it weren't for the officers, the Army would've been tolerable. They left him alone most of the time, which was how he liked it. And then the god-damned officers had kicked him out. They'd made him talk to an Army psychologist, and then they kicked him out. So Major had had it coming.

The lights went out at about eleven o'clock, and he waited another hour and a half before donning the protective suit and gloves and approaching the house. The back door was locked, and he had to pry it open. It opened into the kitchen, and he stepped inside and listened for a good five minutes without moving, to be sure that he hadn't disturbed the occupants, and to allow his eyes to adjust to the lower light level in the house. A little moon light made its way in through the windows, and dim lights shone from control panels on kitchen appliances. It was enough. He heard nothing but the low hum of the refrigerator and the sound of his own breathing. He smelled popcorn.

It was a small house. On the other side of the kitchen was a hallway with a few doors leading off of it, to a bathroom, a living room and a dining room, he presumed. He wasn't interested in any of those rooms. At the end of the hallway was a stairway leading up. He left his bag by the door and moved quietly across the kitchen and down the hall to the stairs, stopping occasionally to listen. He worked his way up the stairs, being careful to step on the outside edges of the treads, so they wouldn't creak. At the top of the stairs was another hallway, heading back in the other direction, with a door opening off of it on each side. The doors of both rooms were open, and soft light shone out of each. Night lights. He stopped again to listen, and now he could hear them breathing. It sounded like the woman was in the room on the right and the child was in the room on the left.

He was correct. The woman lay on her side on the nearer side of a large bed, clutching a pillow, probably the one that was missing from the other side of the bed. She was wearing what looked like a man's red tee shirt with some kind of logo on it, but the bed clothes were pulled up under her left arm, so he couldn't see what kind of logo. Her long brown hair was draped over her pillow.

Before she could wake up, he severed her spine at the base of her skull. In other circumstances, he would've taken his time and enjoyed himself, but he couldn't risk waking the child or alerting the neighbors, if any were home. She was lucky. She'd probably never been hurt in her life, not really hurt, and now she never would be. He hadn't been so lucky. Mother had seen to that.

He'd tried to be as quiet as possible, but the child in the room across the hall must have been woken by the noise, and she called, "Mommy?" He stepped quickly across to her darkened room and killed her with a sharp blow to the side of the head, before she realized that he wasn't her. Another lucky one.

Once they could no longer cry out, he could afford to enjoy himself. It wasn't as satisfying as hurting a living person, but it would have to do. They'd had it too good for too long, and he enjoyed it, but when he tried to smile his face hurt.

He saw now that the logo on the tee shirt was a stylized wolf, and the words read 'New Mexico Lobos.' He'd never heard of them, but he didn't follow sports. The little blonde girl was wearing pajamas covered with pictures of some green, furry creature sticking out of a garbage can. He wondered what the hell that was all about.

Back in the kitchen, he cleaned his weapon at the sink with a scouring sponge. Mother never allowed untidiness. Blood swirled down the drain, and bits of skin, hair and bone collected in the trap. When it was clean, he put it aside, took a dish towel that was draped over the handle of the dishwasher, wet it and used it to gently wipe the blood from his face. Once he'd cleaned up, he removed the white, full-body protective suit he wore over his clothes. It covered everything except his face and his hands, which were encased in disposable rubber gloves. The suit and gloves were spattered with gore. He took the suit off, turned it inside out, and put it in his bag for disposal later. He'd leave the gloves on until he was outside the house. He felt good. Everything had gone without a hitch.

He put his newly cleaned weapon in his bag and left the way he'd come. The boss would pay well for this night's work, but he would've done it for free.

CHAPTER 2

Robbie Bowman saw the police cruiser slow down and pull over, right in front of him. It wasn't the first time he'd been approached by the police. Usually, they'd pull alongside, ask him where he was from and where he was going and suggest – usually politely, sometimes not – that he continue on his way. He never resented it, if they were polite. That was their job, to keep their towns clear of people like him, drifters with no good reason for being there. And, more often than not, continuing on his way was just what he was inclined to do.

But this morning was different. He was already on the outskirts of town, and clearly leaving, so there was no need to urge him on. And they seemed to be more focused, like they were looking for him, rather than happening upon him.

The cruiser stopped abruptly about twenty feet in front of him and both front doors flew open. Two officers were out in an instant, crouching behind their doors with guns drawn and pointed at Bowman.

"Put your hands up and don't move!" shouted the one on the driver's side, who was clearly the older, and in charge. He looked to be in his late forties or early fifties, judging by the lines in his face. He wasn't a big man, but he was wiry and had a weathered, leathery look. That and his white Stetson hat suggested cowboy to Bowman, and he should've been carrying a Colt revolver. But he was holding a Glock 17 pistol, instead, and he appeared to be fully at ease with it.

The order couldn't be taken literally. He could put his hands up or not move, but not both. Bowman put his hands up slowly, then didn't move.

Boss Cop looked fully prepared, even eager, to shoot if Bowman gave him any excuse, but his junior partner worried Bowman more. Junior Cop looked to be in his mid-twenties, had blonde hair and blue eyes, and was a little bigger than average. He had the look of a high school football star a little past his expiration date, fresh-faced, with a body developed by weight training and wind sprints, but allowed to soften over the last few years. What worried Bowman about Junior was that he was visibly nervous.

This was probably the first time he'd pointed his gun at anyone, and he clearly thought of Bowman as a threat. A panicked twitch of the trigger finger would be all it would take to separate Bowman's soul from his body.

Bowman knew that he looked dangerous. He was maybe a couple of years older than Junior Cop, and about the same height at six feet, but he had the lean, taut look usually associated with smaller men. His muscles were formed by hard use and lean living, rather than weight training, and hadn't been allowed to soften. He'd showered and shaved earlier that day, but his light brown hair hadn't seen a barber in months and sprayed out from under his boonie hat and over his ears. His dirty jeans and tee shirt showed obvious signs of wear. His face and arms were sunburned and marked here and there with lighter scar tissue. I look, thought Bowman, like a wild man.

"Drop your pack," ordered Boss Cop.

"Yes sir," Bowman replied, "but I'll need to use my

hands." He wasn't going to give them any excuse to shoot.

"One hand at a time, then, and do it slowly."

Bowman complied, and his backpack fell to the ground behind him. "Now take two steps forward and lay face down, with your hands forward." Once again, Bowman complied.

Once Bowman was down, Boss Cop straightened up and came around from behind the driver's side door, keeping his gun trained on Bowman. "Cuff him, Ken, and put him in the back. If he gives you any trouble, just get out of my line of fire and I'll do the rest."

'Ken,' like Barbie and Ken, Bowman thought. It fit. He suppressed the urge to protest, and concentrated on being cooperative and looking non-threatening. This could all be sorted out later, if he wasn't shot in the meantime.

Deputy Ken came out from behind his door, holstered his gun, another Glock, and retrieved a pair of handcuffs from their case on the back of his belt. Squatting down by Bowman, he pulled his arms behind his back and cuffed them together, tighter than Bowman thought necessary, then patted him down.

"Should I read him his rights, Sheriff?"

"No. We'll do that back at the station. Just put him in the back, then take a quick look in his pack and put it in the trunk."

Once Bowman was cuffed, the Sheriff holstered his gun, then took off his hat and wiped his forehead with his shirt sleeve. His short black hair showed no signs of gray. Above the line of his hat brim his forehead was noticeably lighter, and there were branching lines of lighter skin at the corners of his brown eyes. No sunglasses for this sheriff, mirrored or otherwise. Bowman guessed that the Sheriff would feel naked without his hat, but not the deputy, who was no cowboy. Bowman figured that Deputy Ken must have a white Stetson too – it looked like it was part of the uniform – but he wasn't wearing it now.

The deputy pulled Bowman to his feet and walked him to the back seat of the cruiser. He put his hand on top of Bowman's head, guided him in and shut the door. Bowman saw that his name tag read 'Abbott.' The Sheriff got in the driver's seat while Deputy Abbott was retrieving Bowman's pack.

This kind of reception meant that he was suspected of something far more serious than vagrancy. He'd done nothing wrong, at least not lately, but innocent men had been jailed, or worse, before.

"So what's this all about, Sheriff?" he asked.

"I reckon you know exactly what this is about, son." He didn't turn to face Bowman through the wire mesh separating the front seat from the back as he spoke, but watched Abbott as he went through Bowman's pack. From the back seat, Bowman couldn't see Abbott.

After Abbott had stowed the pack and climbed into the front passenger seat, he turned to Bowman. "That's a wicked weapon you've got!" Abbott's nervousness had been replaced by excitement. The sheriff didn't look surprised, or even particularly interested. He must have seen it and recognized it while Abbot was going through his pack.

"It's a tool," Bowman said.

"A tool, all right," said the sheriff, pulling back onto the road. "A combat knife, a tool designed for killing people."

Bowman said nothing. The sheriff was right. It was a combat knife, but not just any combat knife. The knife is known to the U.S. Army Special Forces as "The Yarborough." To everyone else it was the Green Beret Knife. A serialized version of the knife, with the "Yarborough" name and a serial number inscribed on the blade, is presented to each graduate of the Special Forces Qualification Course. But that wasn't how Bowman got his. He had to buy his, and it wasn't cheap. It did have its peaceful uses. It was sturdy enough to chop wood with, and the seven-inch blade was sharp enough to shave with, but he'd acquired it for its primary purpose. He'd become attached to that knife – it had saved his life once – and saw no reason to leave it behind when he took to the road the previous year. He'd never used it in anger, stateside, but displaying it on his hip had avoided trouble more than once. It scared people, and sometimes that was helpful.

The trip to the police station took only a couple of minutes. It was a one-story brick building with a sign over a pair of glass doors that read, 'Bronco County Sheriff's Dept.' There was one other police vehicle in the parking lot, the police version of the Ford Explorer SUV, with the same words on the side. The car Bowman was in was a Ford Crown Victoria, the old police standard. Bowman had seen a great many police vehicles over the last several months, in various parts of the country, and had noticed that there were not so many Crown Vics as there used to be, and more of the SUVs. He wondered why.

As he was being walked up the short set of steps to the front door, Bowman said, "Don't you have to tell me what I'm being charged with?"

"You haven't been charged with anything yet," said the sheriff. "That isn't up to me. But you've been arrested on suspicion of murder."

Murder certainly was more serious than vagrancy, and that explained the aggressive reception. But he wasn't overly concerned. He was innocent, and the truth would out.

"You're barkin' up the wrong tree, Sheriff. I'm not your man."

"You be sure an' tell that to the judge, son."

Abbott walked Bowman through the glass doors, and the sheriff followed. The central area of the station house was open, with most of it divided into cubicles by chest-high partitions. Enclosed rooms were situated along two of the four walls. One of the cubicles was occupied by a man wearing headphones with an attached microphone, in front of some kind of console. The dispatcher, Bowman figured.

The only other person in the open central area was a middle-aged woman named Rosa Flores, according to the sign on her desk. She was short and a little chubby and looked Hispanic, as the name implied, with dark hair and brown eyes. She wore a small silver cross on a silver chain and reading glasses on a string around her neck. On her desk was a little statue of the Madonna holding the baby Jesus, and what looked like a family photograph. She was in it, together with a man about her age and a young man about Bowman's age.

"Let's take the cuffs off and do the fingerprints first, Ken."

The sheriff stood by, his hand resting casually on the butt of his holstered gun, his finger on the safety strap, while Abbott removed the handcuffs, took Bowman's fingerprints and then put the handcuffs back on.

Once Bowman was safely handcuffed again, the sheriff walked into one of the rooms to the right of the door, near Rosa Flores' cubicle, and left Abbott to process Bowman. A sign on the door of the room read 'Robert Cane, Bronco County Sheriff.' Mrs. Flores must be his secretary.

Abbott took an inventory of Bowman's personal property, which didn't take long. Apart from what he was wearing and his knife, he had some spare clothes, some food and water, some basic toiletries, a small first aid kit, a compass and a paperback book. Mrs. Flores helped Abbott fill out the paperwork. When she spoke, which wasn't often, she did so with a Spanish accent. She was professional enough, but exuded disapproval and disgust. Bowman didn't mind the disapproval much – he'd gotten used to that reaction over the past year – but the disgust bothered him. Most people disapproved of a man who wandered from place to place, with no apparent purpose. It didn't fit the accepted pattern of their orderly world, and it made people uncomfortable. But the disapproval was directed at this eccentric behavior, and he didn't take it personally. The disgust he thought he detected in Mrs. Flores, however, was directed at him personally. She thought he was a murderer, and that pained him.

Cane and Abbott also thought he was a murderer, but that didn't bother him so much, for some reason. Perhaps it was because Mrs. Flores reminded him of his mother, somehow. Not the way she looked, but her mannerisms, perhaps. He couldn't pin down just what it was.

Abbott was also professional, but unlike Mrs. Flores, it wasn't clear from his demeanor what he thought of Bowman. He referred from time to time to a checklist, and Bowman guessed that he hadn't booked many suspects. He was probably only two or three years younger than Bowman, but seemed much younger. Bowman got the sense that Abbott hadn't had much life experience, and was a little naïve. This line of work will cure him of that, if he lives long enough.

When the booking process was finished, Abbott walked Bowman to a holding cell at the back of the police station. There were two sets of bunk beds, one against each side wall, but he was to be the only occupant. A stainless steel toilet and sink against the far wall completed the furnishings. It smelled of disinfectant. The walls and the floor were painted battleship gray, as was the metal door, which had a steel-mesh reinforced window in it at eye level. There was no other window. An orange prison jumpsuit and a pair of paper slippers lay on one of the lower bunks.

"Take your clothes off, sir, and change into that jumpsuit."

"I'd be happy to, but I'm not Houdini," Bowman said, moving his cuffed hands to one side to illustrate the problem.

It appeared to Bowman that Abbott hadn't encountered this problem before, because he had an uncertain, puzzled look on this face. Bowman seemed to be his first customer.

Finally, he said, "OK, turn around and kneel down, sir." When Bowman had done so, he removed the handcuffs and stepped back. "Once you've finished changing, put your clothes by the door and knock on it. I'll be waiting outside."

Bowman changed into the orange jumpsuit and slippers, put his clothes by the door, knocked on it and then sat down on one of the bunks. Abbott looked through the window to see where Bowman was, then opened the door, gathered up the clothes and locked him in.

CHAPTER 3

After he was locked in, Bowman sat on one of the beds, occasionally getting up to pace up and down his cell, and let his mind wander. It was difficult to judge how much time had passed, here in his cell, where there was no sun or any other point of reference.

There was no point in brooding over his current predicament, since there was nothing he could do about it for now, and he didn't even know what precisely he was suspected of doing. Instead, he let one thought lead to another, more or less at random, as he often did when alone on the road.

He thought about the past, mostly, or about subjects outside of himself, but rarely about the future. He'd heard it said that the past is a foreign country, and perhaps that is true for civilization as a whole. But for any given person, it is the future that is a foreign country, distant and unknowable. A person's past, good or bad, is at least known, and there's some comfort in that.

Increasingly, his thoughts turned to food. That meant that it was probably early afternoon. He'd been arrested at about nine in the morning, so call it four hours ago. He'd eaten breakfast at a diner before heading out of town, but was starting to wonder whether lunch would be served when he heard a commotion outside his cell. Someone was very angry and yelling loudly. Bowman couldn't make out any of the words, but he recognized Sheriff Cane's voice replying to the man, in calm but firm tones. The conversation went back and forth for a minute or two – the loud, angry voice and then Cane's calm, firm voice – and then he heard the sound of someone leaving through glass doors in the front, and by the sound of it nearly ripping them off the hinges in the process. A few minutes later Abbott's face appeared at the window in the door.

"Face the opposite wall, sir, and put one hand on each top bunk," he ordered. Once Bowman had done this, he entered the cell and cuffed Bowman's hands behind his back once more. "Somebody wants to talk to you," he said, and led Bowman out of the cell. It felt good to be out of that gray box, even in handcuffs and under guard. Abbot led him back through the central cubicle area of the station to a small room at the other end. Mrs. Flores was the only other person in the central area, apart from the dispatcher, and she gave him her look of disgust. He gave her his sweetest smile, which wasn't sweet enough to soften her expression. She turned away, making the sign of the cross, head, heart, shoulder, shoulder, to ward off evil. It hurt him to see it, and his smile faded.

The room to which Abbott led him contained a metal table about six feet long, extending from the door towards the far wall, and two metal chairs, one on either end of the table. The walls were bare except for a mirror built into the left wall. In the far chair sat a small, dark-haired, olive-skinned man in a gray suit, white shirt and blue tie. A matching blue pocket square protruded from his breast pocket. Behind him and a little to the side stood a large black man in gray slacks, an open-collared white shirt and a blue blazer. He looked like he could've been a linebacker in his youth, but had softened and settled a bit in middle age. Abbott walked Bowman to the nearer chair, shackled his left leg to the table leg – there were shackles in place for the purpose – and removed the handcuffs.

"You want me to stay, sir?" said Abbott to the man in the suit.

"No. Thank you, Deputy Abbott. I will call you if I need you. And it is 'detective,' not 'sir.'" He spoke with a preciseness that suggested to Bowman that English wasn't his first language.

"Right, sir," said Abbott. "Detective, I mean."

After Abbott left, the detective pulled a manila folder from a black briefcase at the side of his chair and put it on the table in front of him. He pulled a pair of wire-rimmed glasses from an inside pocket of his suit jacket, put them on, and started to flip through the papers inside. Without looking up from the papers, he said, "I am Detective Carrillo of the New Mexico State Police, and this is my colleague, Detective Paine. Have you been read your Miranda rights?" He pronounced 'Miranda' and his own name in the Spanish fashion, but otherwise there was no detectable accent.

"No, sir," said Bowman. "Detective, I mean."

Carrillo looked up from his papers and removed his glasses. He wasn't smiling. "I think perhaps you do not appreciate the seriousness of your situation, Mr. Bowman."

Perhaps I don't, Bowman thought. "What is my situation, Detective?"

"I will tell you, but first I must read you your rights." He pulled a laminated card from an inside pocket of his jacket, put his glasses back on, and read from it. "You have the right to remain silent. Anything you say or do can and will be used against you in a court of law. You have the right to consult an attorney before speaking to the police and to have an attorney present during questioning now or in the future. If you cannot afford an attorney, one will be appointed for you before any questioning, if you wish. If you decide to answer any questions now, without an attorney present, you will still have the right to stop answering at any time until you talk to an attorney. Do you understand these rights as I have explained them to you, Mr. Bowman?"

"Yes, I do."

"Very well. I will explain to you the situation in which you find yourself." He briefly consulted his papers and continued, "Yesterday evening, at approximately seven p.m., you checked in to the Western Motel on Main Street, arriving on foot and with no baggage other than your backpack. You paid cash in advance for one night." Carrillo didn't appear to be looking for confirmation, so Bowman offered none. "At approximately eight p.m. you were seen eating at Hank's Diner, also on Main Street. Again, you paid in cash."

"You've done your homework, Detective."

Ignoring Bowman's interruption, Carrillo continued, "At some time between eleven p.m. last night and two a.m. this morning, at a house a short walk from the Western Motel, a young wife and mother named Mary Walker and her three-year-old daughter Emma were murdered."

Bowman felt the blood draining from his face. He felt cold and clammy. This couldn't be happening.

"They were killed with a heavy, edged weapon," Carrillo said.

"Something like that big ol' combat knife of yours," said Paine, breaking his silence. Paine began to pace back and forth behind Carrillo, alternately looking at the floor and then at Bowman. He looked angry.

"The murders were quite brutal," Carrillo continued, seeming not to notice Paine's interjection. "Many of the wounds, and there were a great many, were inflicted after death. The killer seems to have been very angry, or perhaps he derived some perverse pleasure from the attack."

"Yeah, you one sick son of a bitch," said Paine, glaring at Bowman. Bowman fought down the urge to respond.

That would be just what Paine wanted.

Carrillo paused briefly, studying Bowman, and then continued, "Or perhaps the killer wanted to send a message of some kind."

Bowman fought the urge to vomit. How could this be? What were the odds?

With an effort, Bowman pulled himself together, laid his hands flat on the table in front of him and drew a deep breath. "You have my attention now, Detective, but you've got the wrong man. You said earlier that I have a right to legal counsel. I want a lawyer before this goes any further."

"That is indeed your right, Mr. Bowman. Are you expecting your friends to supply you with an attorney?"

"Nobody's come to help you yet," Paine said. "They probably left you here to rot."

"My friends? No friend of mine even knows what part of the country I'm in."

"Business associates, then?" said Carrillo. "El Chato, perhaps?"

"Is that supposed to mean something to me, Detective?"

Carrillo put his fingertips together under his chin and studied Bowman's face for what seemed to Bowman a long time, but was probably only few seconds. Bowman wondered what he was looking for.

"Am I correct, then, in presuming that you are a man of limited means and will require the State to appoint counsel for you?"

"Yes, Detective. 'A man of limited means' describes me perfectly." He had been called worse.

Carrillo took another few seconds to consider this, while Paine continued to pace back and forth in the background, alternately looking at the floor or casting angry glances at Bowman. Bowman's lack of means seemed to signify more to Carrillo than Bowman thought it should. Finally, he said, "Legal counsel can be found for you, of course, and you may refuse to speak to me in the interim. But Tierra Roja is a small town, and no lawyer with the appropriate expertise is available locally. We will need to bring in a lawyer from some hours away. It may be a matter of days. In the meantime, you will be remanded to the State Penitentiary at Santa Fe. A small town such as Tierra Roja has neither the facilities nor the personnel necessary to keep a person in custody for so long."

"Oh, they gonna love you at the State Pen," said Paine. "See, even gang bangers got a code. They don't like folks that hurt kids. You gonna need to watch your back." Bowman always did, but Paine had made his point.

Once again, Carrillo seemed not to notice Paine's interruption, and he continued, "We will wait with you here while transportation to Santa Fe is being arranged."

Carrillo nodded at the mirror to his right, to Cane or Abbott, Bowman presumed, who would make the arrangements. They then lapsed into silence. Carrillo sat looking impassively at Bowman; Paine paced back and forth behind him, looking down at the floor. Bowman shifted his gaze from one to the other, then to the table top in front of him. No matter where he was looking, he could feel Carrillo's gaze upon him. It was an uncomfortable feeling, far worse than the angry looks from Paine. Carrillo seemed to be looking right through him. And the combination of Carrillo's infinite patience and Paine's impatient pacing grated on Bowman's nerves. Time passed, how much he didn't know, and still Paine paced and Carrillo gazed. How much longer would he have to wait?

Maybe he didn't need a lawyer.

Bowman knew that innocent men were convicted by their own statements from time to time, perhaps more often than he guessed. He'd seen enough crime dramas to know that his smartest move was to wait for a lawyer, even if it meant spending more time in custody and a trip to the

State Penitentiary. But he'd become accustomed lately to having lots of room to move around in, and the last few hours locked in the small cell had been trying. The thought of even more time behind bars caused his gut to twist uncomfortably. He knew that Carrillo couldn't connect him physically to the crime scene, because he hadn't been there. While Bowman could understand why he was a suspect, there appeared to be no evidence against him beyond the coincidence of his arriving in town at the wrong time, looking the part and possessing a plausible murder weapon.

"OK, Detective, let's give this a try. But the questions stop when I say so."

Paine stopped pacing, turned towards Bowman and smiled smugly. He and Carrillo had won the first round, and he seemed confident that they'd win the match as well.

"Of course, Mr. Bowman," said Carrillo, without any trace of the gloating so evident in Paine's manner. "Please understand that our conversation is being recorded."

"I had guessed," said Bowman, glancing at the mirror.

"First, Mr. Bowman, I ask that you confirm that you have knowingly and voluntarily waived your right to counsel, and that you consent to answer our questions without an attorney present on your behalf. Is that correct?"

"Yes."

"Thank you. For the record, please state your full name and place of residence."

"My name is Robert Roy Bowman. I don't currently have a place of residence."

"Your driver's license, Mr. Bowman, shows your address as Page, Montana. Is that your last place of residence?"

"Yes, and where I was born and raised."

"When did you leave that place?"

"About a year ago, last June. Shortly after I was discharged from the Army."

"Ah yes, the Army. You have an impressive record, Mr. Bowman," said Carrillo, consulting the papers in his folder. "Eight years in the service, one tour of duty in Iraq, another two in Afghanistan. A Purple Heart and a Bronze Star. You received an honorable discharge with the rank of Corporal. With that record, I am surprised that you were not promoted to Sergeant."

"I'm not surprised," said Paine with a snort, and Bowman shot him an angry look.

None of Paine's interjections had been in the form of a question, and he seemed to be there just to provoke or unsettle him. Bowman decided to follow Carrillo's lead and just ignore Paine, if he could.

"They offered, but I wasn't buying. Too much responsibility. I might have stayed in longer, but it was up or out, and I chose out. The Army loves old Sergeants, but not old Corporals."

"Old, Mr. Bowman? I believe you are only twenty-seven."

"Like I said, old."

"Yeah, you a regular octogenarian," said Paine, enunciating the last word like he was offering it up at a spelling bee. Bowman guessed that Paine's rough manner and language was just part of his bad cop act. The character he was playing would not have used a word like 'octogenarian.' And that character would not have risen to the level of detective, either. Beat cop, maybe, but not homicide detective. Paine was starting to extend the range of his pacing, no longer limiting himself to the area behind Carrillo, but moving up and down either side of the table as well. It was distracting, as he was sure it was intended to be.

"So you were discharged and you returned to your home town in Montana, if only briefly," Carrillo said, ignoring Paine. "Why did you leave Montana?"

"There was nothing there for me anymore."

"How do you mean, Mr. Bowman?"

"Well, my parents had died while I was overseas, in a car accident, and I don't have any other family in the area. My friends from when I was growing up were all moved away, or . . ." Bowman paused.

After a few moments, Carrillo said, almost gently, "Or what, Mr. Bowman?"

"Or they saw how fucked in the head you was, I bet, and didn't want to hang with you no more," said Paine, who was now behind Bowman and leaning in close to his ear. Bowman turned sharply and glared at Paine, who straightened up, put his hands up and his innocent face on, as if to say, 'who, me?' and took a step back. "Sorry, my man, did I touch a nerve?"

Paine had touched a nerve. He had found a nerve and ground his heel in it. Just standing behind him had made him intensely uncomfortable, and the comment had hit home. But Bowman knew he had to calm down and not react to Paine's game.

He turned his eyes back to the table in front of him and thought about his attempts to renew old friendships after eight years of living a life that none of his childhood friends could understand. They'd tried to understand, of course. They were good people, and could see that he had changed somehow. But they didn't know how to talk to him, and he didn't know how to talk to them. And Bowman didn't make it easy for them. He had been too quick to anger, always on edge. He hadn't liked the man he was starting to become, and felt the need for some space to sort it out.

He saw the world differently now, in a way that they could never understand. He saw it more clearly, he thought. He'd peeled away some layers, and what was underneath seemed more real. He'd seen man at his most brutal, but he'd also seen sacrifice and loyalty. He couldn't bring himself to care about the things that his hometown friends cared about, that he had once cared about, like whether the Grizzlies beat the Bobcats. But he wasn't sure what he did care about now.

Yet Bowman wasn't going to share any of those thoughts with Carrillo and Paine. He'd sound like damaged goods, just the kind of guy that would snap and carve up a couple of innocents.

"You were saying that your friends had all moved away or – or what?"

"Or married, Detective. Married guys just don't want to hang around with single guys. My old friends, those who were still around, were married and starting families. I guess I was the odd man out."

"Yeah, right," said Paine, rolling his eyes dramatically.

"I see," said Carrillo, but Bowman thought that Carrillo understood more than he let on. "Your military record shows that you once sought the treatment of a psychologist. What was troubling you, Mr. Bowman?"

Bowman colored. "They told me that was confidential," he said angrily.

"What you said to the psychologist is confidential, but the fact that you spoke with him is not. You can, of course, tell me what it was about."

"This should be good," said Paine.

Bowman hesitated. He could make something up, but he suspected that Carrillo was good at recognizing lies. He couldn't tell the truth. No one would believe it was just a coincidence. Finally, he said, "No, Detective, I'd rather not."

"Now that's a surprise," said Paine, who was clearly not surprised. Bowman shot him a dark look, but said nothing.

Carrillo pulled a cloth from an inside pocket of his jacket and began to polish his glasses. He let the silence lengthen and grow uncomfortable. Bowman would even have welcomed a snide comment from Paine, but Paine kept silent as well. After what seemed to Bowman like an eternity, Carrillo said, "Perhaps you will tell me this much, Mr. Bowman. Did it have to do with your attitude towards women?"

Bowman was relieved to be past the awkward silence, but both startled and puzzled by the question. Because it did have to do with women, or rather a woman and a girl. But not his 'attitude towards women.'

"My attitude towards women? What do you mean? No, no it didn't."

After a short pause, Carrillo said, "Thank you. We will move on. So you decided to leave your home town. Where did you go?"

"Well, I started out going east, through the Dakotas, Minnesota and Wisconsin. When it started to get cold, I headed south, to Illinois, Missouri, Arkansas and Texas. Now I'm in New Mexico."

"And what is your final destination?"

Good question, Bowman thought. That's just what he himself would love to know.

"I don't know. Maybe I'll know the place when I see it. Most places don't encourage a trial residence, so I keep moving. Sometimes I take a bus, sometimes I hitch a ride, mostly I walk."

"And how do you live, Mr. Bowman? I mean, what do you do for money?"

"I have some savings in a bank back in Montana, what my parents left me and what I've saved on my own. I can draw from that with my ATM card, and I do odd jobs from time to time. I don't need much. Occasionally I'll spring for a room and a shower, but I'm not afraid to sleep in the rough."

"I bet one of your 'odd jobs' brought you here to Tierra Roja," said Paine, who was now back on the other side of the room, behind Carrillo.

This latest jab from Paine finally tripped some switch in Bowman's mind. He jumped up from his chair, pounded his balled fists on the table and exploded, "Oh for Christ's sake! Do I look like a monster to you?"

The door behind Bowman flew open and Abbott ran

in, stopping short once he saw that Bowman was only standing, glaring at Paine, who was glaring right back. Abbott looked from Bowman to Carrillo, awaiting instructions.

"In my experience, Mr. Bowman, monsters look much like the rest of us," Carrillo said. To Abbott, he said, "Thank you, Deputy, but your assistance is not needed at present. You will recall that you took the precaution of shackling Mr. Bowman's leg to the table, so we are in no danger. And Mr. Bowman's demonstration was quite justified. My colleague had insulted him, though without meaning to, I'm sure, and for that I apologize." He nodded his head in Bowman's direction. "Please be seated, Mr. Bowman. Thank you again, Deputy Abbott, I will let you know if I need you."

Bowman slumped back in his chair and dropped his gaze to the table as Abbott left, to go back to the observation room on the other side of the mirror, Bowman presumed. He had let Paine rattle him, get him to shout something out without thinking, to sound defensive. He needed to calm down and be more careful.

"Let us continue, Mr. Bowman," said Carrillo, after a few moments. "Did you have a purpose for coming to Tierra Roja?"

"No, apart from the fact that it was between where I was and where I was going."

"And where were you going?"

"Like I said, maybe I'll know when I get there."

"Oh, I get it," said Paine sarcastically, throwing his hands in the air and looking heavenward, "you trying to 'find yourself,' like some goddamned hippie."

Not myself, thought Bowman, but said nothing.

"I understand," said Carrillo, ignoring Paine. "Please tell me exactly what you did from the time you arrived in Tierra Roja until the time you were arrested."

"There's not much to tell. I walked into town after my last ride had dropped me off a few miles up the road, and decided I was due for a bed, a shower and a hot meal."

"I bet you was due for a shower, all right," said Paine.

"Your last ride? Can you identify the person or car? Perhaps that person could corroborate your story."

"He will if you can find him. Guy's name was Ben, I think. I only got the one name. He was driving a white pickup truck, not new. New Mexico plates, I think. He picked me up about a hundred miles down the highway and let me off here 'cause he was going off to the south and I wanted to keep going west."

Bowman could've told Carrillo a lot more about Ben, his hobbies, his love life, which sports teams he liked, and what kind of mileage he got from his truck. Ben liked to talk, as did most people who stopped to give Bowman a ride, and Bowman didn't mind listening. It was a small price to pay for a ride, and he found most people interesting, each in his own way.

"Thank you, but that is not much to go on."

"Well, he gave me a book. Maybe he wrote his name in it. It was in my pack."

"Ah yes, Moby Dick. I read it many years ago. I think you will enjoy it, Mr. Bowman. We will look for any name written in it, but I don't remember seeing any. Please continue."

"Moby Dick? Shit, I bet you ain't never read a book didn't have pictures in it."

Bowman was beginning to find Paine more amusing than intimidating.

"So I checked into the motel, as you know. I showered in my room and then walked over to the diner to get something to eat. After that I walked down Main Street a little to see what the town had to offer. There wasn't much to see, so I was back in my room by nine or nine thirty. I read my book for a little bit and then went to sleep. In the morning, this morning, I got up, shaved, showered and hit the road. I ate breakfast at the same diner and was walking out of town, going west, when I was arrested."

"Can anyone corroborate any part of your story, Mr. Bowman?"

Paine contributed his usual snort, and said, "Not likely."

Bowman shrugged. "Just the parts you already know about, I guess. Checking in to the motel – the diner."

"Let us talk about your knife, Mr. Bowman. Where did you get it, and why do you carry it?"

"I bought it while I was in Afghanistan. A lot of us wanted something better than the standard-issue combat utility knife, and that knife is supposed to be the best. And it's intimidating. Afghan culture is a warrior culture, and they respect blades."

"I bet you like to intimidate people," said Paine, from behind Bowman, who pointedly ignored him.

"And why do you carry this weapon of war now that you are no longer at war?"

"Because I own it, Detective, and I carry everything I own. And it's useful. I do a lot of camping."

"Camping?" said Paine, rolling his eyes again.

"Have you ever been in trouble with the law before, Mr. Bowman?"

Bowman thought about that. He and a group of his buddies had been rounded up by the military police once for drunk and disorderly, for having too much fun at a local bar near the base. Boone had been with him, of course. Where you found Bowman, you found Boone, and vice versa. Their friends called them Bowman and Boone, because it sounded better than Boone and Bowman, better rhythm to it, but it was usually Boone that led the way into whatever trouble they found themselves in. They'd had to spend the night in the stockade, but no charges had ever been filed. He decided that didn't count. He'd been approached by the civilian police numerous times since he got out of the service, and sometimes they'd given him a free ride out of town, but he'd never been arrested before now.

"No. I try to keep my nose clean."

Paine snorted.

"You said earlier that you had no family in the area of Page, Montana, your home town. Do you have any family, anywhere?"

"I – I don't know."

"You don't know, Mr. Bowman?"

"I had a sister, Bridget, who was a few years older than me. She ran away from home when I was in high school, and we haven't heard from her since. We – I – don't know where she is, or if she's even alive."

Bowman braced for a wisecrack from Paine, but it didn't come. So the man does have a soul, he thought. All three were silent for a while.

"The young red-headed girl in the photograph?"

Bowman glared at Carrillo. The thought of them going through his belongings had not really bothered him until then, but now he felt violated and resented it deeply.

Carrillo dropped his eyes briefly, acknowledging the resentment and perhaps the justice of it. When he raised them again, he said, "I invade your privacy only because duty requires it. I wish it did not."

Now it was Bowman's turn to drop his gaze, and his resentment evaporated.

"Yes, that's her. You asked me earlier if I had a purpose in coming here, and what I told you wasn't the whole truth. I came here looking for Bridget."

"Do you have reason to believe she might be here?"

"No. I have no idea where she is, so it doesn't much matter where I look for her." The truth was that he wasn't doing anything differently than he would have if he weren't looking for Bridget, but it gave him a sense of purpose. And that helped a little.

After another long silence, Carrillo put his glasses on and flipped through his papers for a minute or two, considering, and then, without consulting with Paine, or so much as looking at him, he looked up and said, "I think that will be all for now, Mr. Bowman."

"For now?"

"Yes. The State Police laboratory has not finished examining your personal property. Depending upon what they find, I may have further questions for you."

Carrillo nodded at the mirror, and in a few moments Abbott came through the door and motioned for Bowman to stand up to be handcuffed.

"So what happens next?" Bowman asked Carrillo, as Abbott handcuffed him and released the leg shackle.

"With certain exceptions, the law requires that we charge you or release you within twenty-four hours." Bowman wondered if one such exception had to do with waiting for legal counsel, or if Carrillo had been bluffing about sending him to the State Penitentiary. "You will know one way or the other no later than tomorrow morning."

Abbott led him back to his cell and locked him in, without a word.

The heavy metal door clanged shut, and the sound reverberated in the small, gray room.

Bowman felt drained, and lay down on one of the lower bunks to consider what had just happened and what he'd learned. Being accused of killing the woman and child had hit much too close to home, and it had rattled him.

CHAPTER 4

Anbar Province, Republic of Iraq (2007)

"Too fucking hot in this goddamn country," said Jackson, from about ten meters behind Bowman.

Bowman didn't turn to look back. He was the team leader for the front fire team, and therefore point man for the entire squad, and had to keep his eyes forward. They were patrolling the streets around the fire base, to show the flag and to provide a target for the insurgents. The only way to find them was to let them attack you.

Cedric ("Ace") Jackson, as the grenadier of his fire team, had an M203 grenade launcher slung under the barrel of his rifle and was second in the file, followed by Murphy, with his M249 Squad Automatic Weapon. Clayton Boone brought of the rear of his four-man fire team, and he was followed by Sergeant Petrosyan, the squad leader, and then the rear fire team. They were staggered, left and right, as much as the width of the street would allow, and strung out over about ninety meters.

"You should be used to this, Ace. Iraq can't be any hotter'n Mississippi," said Murphy.

"Yeah, Mississippi's too fucking hot too, but at least I

ain't luggin' seventy pounds of armor and shit around when I'm home. Bet it's nice and cool up in Montana, ain't it Robbie?"

"Sure is, Ace. A constant sixty-five degrees and sunny, even at night."

Jackson and Murphy chuckled. Bowman couldn't keep up with their constant chatter, but they liked to bring him into the conversation now and then, usually as a kind of neutral referee.

As they walked, Bowman blinked the sweat out of his eyes and surveyed the street ahead, a dirty brown track flanked by dirty grey buildings and an occasional palm tree. The palm trees had surprised him at first. He had always associated them with white-sand tropical beaches and frozen daiquiris. Not anymore. But what he noticed most now was something that wasn't there. The street was empty, and that was never a good sign.

"Trouble with you, Ace, is that you're a complainer," said Murphy. "Iraq has many fine features. It's got more sand than you can shake a stick at, and a fine assortment of goats."

"Yeah, I know you like the goats, Murph. I saw you eyeing that cute one 'bout half a click back."

"Now that was a handsome goat, but it had a set of balls on it that would do any of us proud. That might not matter to you, but I have standards to maintain. It just wouldn't be right."

Bowman smiled. They could go on like this for hours, and sometimes did.

Jackson was just starting his reply when the dust in the street began to dance and the air was filled with the chatter of small arms fire.

"Incoming!" yelled Bowman, and every man in the squad sprinted for the nearest cover, on either side of the street.

"Fuck! I'm hit!" yelled Jackson.

From the shelter of a doorway, Bowman looked back

to see Jackson on the ground in the middle of the street, clutching at his leg and working his way through his extensive vocabulary of curse words with a will. Bowman ran towards Jackson and saw that Murphy was running towards him as well, from the opposite direction. They reached him at about the same time, grabbed him by his shoulder straps and dragged him to the side of the street as AK-47 rounds kicked up dirt around them. Bowman was almost used to being shot at by now. Almost.

In a small, sheltered courtyard Bowman and Murphy propped Ace up in a sitting position with his back against a wall and paused to catch their breath and settle their nerves. They were as fit as they had ever been in their lives, but with the weight of their own body armor and other gear, and dragging Jackson and all his, it had been exhausting. The adrenaline rush had gotten him through it, but you can't just turn it off when it's no longer needed. His hands were shaking.

Jackson's leg was bleeding, but didn't look too bad. If the bullet had hit a major artery the blood would be spraying out of the wound. Bowman left Murphy to bandage the wound and headed back to the edge of the street.

Behind him, he heard Jackson say, "Easy with that shit, you goddamn mick. It fucking hurts."

"See, this is what I've been saying, Ace. You are a complainer."

Glancing back, Bowman saw that Murphy's hands were shaking as well, and he was having trouble with the bandage.

From across the street and a little way back, Sergeant Petrosyan shouted, "Anyone with eyes on?"

Boone, also across the street, but a little forward of Petrosyan, said, "Second floor window, about fifty meters ahead on the left, above the blue door."

"Bowman," Sergeant Petrosyan shouted, "how's Jackson?"

"Took one in the right leg, Sarge, but isn't bleeding too badly. I think he'll keep for a little while."

"Good. I want you and Boone to go flush that bastard out. Wait till Murphy's in position. Rear fire team will move up for area security."

Petrosyan meant that Murphy would provide covering fire with his SAW, while Bowman and Boone approached the target house, which was on Bowman's side of the street. The rest of the squad would support, but Bowman and Boone would be the point of the spear.

The first step was to get Boone across the street to Bowman and send Murphy to the other side, where he would have a better angle on the second floor window from which the shots had been fired. Boone went first, and made it across to Bowman without drawing any fire. That put Bowman, Boone, Murphy and Ace on the same side, in the small courtyard.

"Hey Boone," Murphy said, looking up from bandaging Jackson's leg, "I been meaning to ask you. You related to Daniel Boone?"

Bowman noticed that Murphy's hands were no longer shaking, and his voice was less strained. His own hands had calmed down as well.

"Yes I am, Murph. A direct descendent, on my Daddy's side, of course, along with a smattering of Davy Crockett and some Andrew Jackson. On my Mama's side I'm descended from George Washington and Abraham Lincoln."

"I don't know about them others," Ace said, between grunts of pain, "but I'm pretty sure George Washington didn't have no goddamn kids."

"Even so, Ace, even so."

Bowman smiled to himself, despite their current troubles. He had heard versions of this before, and he was pretty sure Murphy and Jacksons had as well, but the list of Boone's illustrious ancestors was never exactly the same. Depending on the day, they included Jeremiah Johnson,

Captain Kidd and Ethan Allen. So the question was often asked, just to see what the answer would be that day.

The trash talk had settled them all down a little, which was probably Murphy's intention.

"Whenever you're ready, Murph," Bowman said. "I think your best angle to cover us will be just across the street here, behind that low wall."

Murphy finished tying off the bandage he was applying to Jackson's leg, picked up his SAW and joined Bowman and Boone at the edge of the street. He looked at the position that Bowman had recommended and nodded.

"Here goes nothin'," he said, and sprinted across the street.

This time the shooter was ready and managed to get off a burst. One of the rounds knocked Murphy down, but he rolled quickly to the far side of the street and out of the line of fire.

"Murphy, you hit?" shouted Sergeant Petrosyan.

After Murphy had made it to the other side, Bowman had looked over at Jackson and now he saw his face suddenly go tense when he heard the Sergeant's question.

"I'm OK, Sarge," Murphy called. "Got me in the side plate. Just need a minute to catch my breath."

Jackson's face relaxed, and he exhaled loudly. They were all brothers, but some bonds were tighter than others. Bowman had a similar bond with Boone, so he thought he knew something of what Jackson must be feeling.

And he knew why Murphy needed a minute to catch his breath. His body armor had prevented the bullet from penetrating, but a 7.62 millimeter AK-47 round carries a lot of energy, and all that energy got dumped on Murphy. It was like getting kicked by a mule. He would have a nasty bruise, and perhaps a broken rib or two.

While Boone and Bowman waited for Murphy to set up and give them the signal, they checked and rechecked their equipment. Fire selector set on auto, which for their M-4 carbines meant a three-round burst, magazine fully seated, a round in the chamber, spare mags in their proper place. Bowman noticed Boone pat his chest at the base of his neck, as he always did at times like this. He was checking to make sure that the little gold Jesus his mother had sent him was still there. It was not the Jesus dying in torment on the cross, but the living Jesus, with his arms outstretched in welcome or in blessing, like the Christ the Redeemer statue in Rio de Janeiro. Boone had said that he wasn't convinced that it would keep him from harm, as his mother claimed, but it couldn't hurt. Bowman wished he had one of his own.

"How you doin', Ace?" said Boone, talking to Jackson but keeping his eyes on Murphy across the street.

"I don't wanna complain, Boone, but I'll feel a lot better when you boys bring me that cock sucking motherfucker's head."

"We'll see what we can do."

Murphy had pulled himself together and was now ready. He gave them the thumbs up and then opened fire on the window down the street. The SAW was basically a light machine gun, and its high rate of fire usually persuaded anyone on the wrong end of it to keep his head down. As soon as Murphy started shooting, Bowman and Boone sprinted down the street to the blue door and paused next to it with their backs against the wall.

The next part never got any easier. Bowman's heart raced and his mouth was dry. On the other side of this door was a man with a gun, or maybe more than one, who wanted to kill them. Once he went through that door, there would be no room for fear. He would be focused and in the moment. It was the pause before the action that was the hardest, mentally. And delay wouldn't make it any easier. With a nod towards Boone, Bowman stepped away from the wall, turned towards the door and kicked it in. Boone rushed in, followed by Bowman.

Boone moved quickly to the left of the door and Bowman, just behind him, moved to the right, each with his rifle up and scanning. There was no one on the ground floor, which consisted of one large room. It looked lived in, but was unoccupied at the moment. On the side of the room to their right was an open stairway against the wall, leading up to the second floor and back towards the front of the house. The shooter upstairs may have seen them run down the street, and had almost certainly heard them kick in the front door. He'd be waiting for them as they came up the stairs.

Using hand signals to communicate and coordinate their actions, Bowman and Boone moved to the stairs, scanning with their rifles as they went. The top of the stairs opened into a short hallway running in the same direction. From below, they could see the top of a door frame leading to an upstairs room to the right of the hallway. The rest of the door frame and most of the hallway were screened from their view.

Bowman hated stairs. The shooter could be lying or crouched low in the upstairs hallway, ready to shoot off the tops of their heads as soon as they appeared. It was best to expose yourself suddenly, rather than gradually, and only when you could see, and were ready to engage. Bowman motioned for Boone to hang back, and then started slowly up the stairs in a crouch. After a few steps, he stood up straight, his rifle at the ready, and saw that the shooter was crouched just inside the upstairs room, peering out at the head of the stairs over the barrel of an AK-47. Bowman fired first, a three-round burst, and the man quickly pulled back and scrambled deeper into the room. Bowman ran up the stairs, with Boone right behind him.

They squatted with their backs against the concrete wall next to the open door to catch their breath and consider their next move. Bowman was blinking almost continuously now, to keep the sweat out of his eyes. He was not going take a hand from his rifle to wipe his brow. Boone had been the first through the door downstairs, so it was Bowman's turn to go in first now. But the shooter had the door covered, and was waiting for them. It was hard to rush into a room when you feared that you might be running into a buzz saw. It was harder when you knew you would be. But there was an alternative. Bowman touched one of the grenades hanging from the webbing at his chest and looked at Boone, who nodded. Bowman pulled the grenade free, drew the pin, released the lever and counted to two in his head. Then he reached over and tossed the grenade into the room and quickly pulled his hand back as a burst of AK-47 rounds splintered the door frame. He heard frantic scrambling and high-pitched screaming — too high-pitched — and then the grenade exploded and he was up and through door, with Boone right behind him.

The shooter was clearly dead, slumped against the wall opposite the door, mouth open and eyes staring at the ceiling. He had taken the bulk of the blast, and was a bloody, tattered mess. But he hadn't been the only one in the room. In the far corner, on a sleeping mat, were a young woman and a little girl clutching each other. Their colorful dresses were stained with blood, but their faces were unmarred. They were both quite pretty, with dark black hair, honey-colored skin and delicate features, and they looked like they could be sleeping.

"Shit, shit, shit," Bowman whispered. He dropped his rifle and ran over to them. Dropping on his knees, he checked the woman for a pulse and found none. "Son of a bitch!"

As he turned his attention to the girl, her eyes fluttered open, and Bowman's heart leapt. Her dark eyes seemed to look straight through him for a brief moment, and then the light and the life drained out of them as he watched. There was no need to check for a pulse. She was gone.

Bowman's head drooped, and he shook it slowly from side to side, trying to deny the undeniable.

"It ain't your fault, Robbie," Boone said softly, putting

his hand on Bowman's shoulder. "I'd have done the same thing. How could we have known?"

A couple of hours later, back at the fire base, the Lieutenant said something similar, and suggested that Bowman talk to the Army psychologist. So he talked to the psychologist, who said the same thing all over again. The one to blame was the man who had fired at them from a room with civilians in it. That's what they all said. Bowman never learned whether the shooter was related to the woman and child, a husband and father perhaps, or had invaded their home to use it as a fighting position. It didn't really matter. They were dead, and he had killed them.

CHAPTER 5

Bowman awoke in his cell with a start, in a cold sweat. The dreams were still vivid in his mind. They were never exactly the same, but certain sounds, smells and images recurred. The deafening roar of an IED exploding under the Humvee ahead of him, the mushrooming red flames mixed with oily black smoke. The smell of burning rubber, and of burning flesh. Bright red blood, so much blood. The chatter of small arms fire and the whoosh of RPGs. Screams of pain and rage. And the faces. Always the dead, staring faces.

He shook his head to clear it of the horrid images and brought himself back to the here and now. It was the middle of the night, and he was on one of the lower beds in his cell at the Bronco County Sheriff's Department. He knew from experience that it would be useless to try to get back to sleep for some time, so he lay in the dark and let his mind wander back over the last couple of days.

Could it really be nothing more than a chilling coincidence that he'd been accused of something so similar to what he'd actually done, back in Iraq? But of course that was exactly what it was, for what else could it be? Some sort of cosmic justice tracking him down, the hand of providence?

Bowman didn't think he believed in that sort of thing, but it was unsettling. Even if he himself were cleared, he would feel better if he knew who had done the killing, and why.

The woman and child had been murdered while he was in town. As an outsider and a drifter, he was an obvious suspect. But Carrillo and Paine seemed to think that Bowman, or rather whoever the killer was, had 'friends' or 'business associates' who could be expected to help him, and they'd mentioned someone, or something, perhaps, called El Chato. Did they think it was a murder-for-hire? But who would pay for the murder of a young woman and a child, and why in a 'brutal' manner, as Carrillo had put it? Bowman thought that a professional killer would not be emotionally invested, or enraged. Perhaps he was a sadist, as Carrillo had suggested, and got into that line of work to satisfy his urges. Carrillo had suggested something else as well, that perhaps the killer was sending a message. But what kind of message, and to whom?

Bowman had told Carrillo the truth, and nothing but the truth, but he hadn't told him the whole truth. He hadn't mentioned an incident that had happened just after Ben had dropped him off, right before he walked into Tierra Roja. He'd been left at a little roadside place that was a combination gas station and convenience store. Not one of those modern chain stores, but a place that looked like it had been there a hundred years and hadn't been painted in fifty. The gas pumps looked like they'd been installed around the time it was last painted. There were old metal signs tacked to the side of the building advertising various brands of oil, beer and cigarettes, some of which hadn't been sold in years, like Esso oil and Chesterfield cigarettes, and but he didn't see any sign identifying the store.

An old, rusty pick-up truck was parked on the side of the building. Bowman figured that it belonged to the proprietor, since it matched the décor. Out front was a late model black sport utility vehicle, with a serious suspension and large, off-road tires. Judging by the coat of dirt, it had been off the road a lot, and recently.

Bowman didn't know when he would next have a chance to buy something to eat, so he decided to replenish his stock. He stepped in through a screen door, which set off a little bell above it. The proprietor stood behind a counter to the left. On the counter was an old-fashioned cash register, the kind that actually rang when you pulled the handle to ring up a sale, and behind it were a few shelves of the more valuable, and portable, items in stock, such as cigarettes, batteries and so on. To the right were a couple of aisles containing the remaining stock, snacks, motor oil and what seemed to Bowman like a random assortment of other items, including a child's sticker book and some toilet plungers. At the end of the row was a glass-doored cooler full of soft drinks and beer. At the back of the store, opposite the screen door, were a couple of tables and a few folding chairs. Sitting at one of the tables, each with a beer in hand or on the table in front of him, were four men.

The first thing he noticed was their hands, where they were, what was in them. It was a habit now, like crossing the street if he saw a suspicious pile of garbage ahead, something that could conceal an IED. He didn't really think there was any risk, and he didn't do it consciously, but he would often catch himself doing it. Would he always do that? He thought that he was a little more relaxed now than he had been a year ago, so he had reason to hope that it would continue to get better. But in the meantime, this seemed like a good time to be alert and suspicious.

He could tell at a glance that the men at the table were all ex-military. They sized him up quickly, and he was sure they recognized the same thing in him. They didn't wear any kind of uniform, but all were dressed similarly, in tan or green cargo pants, web belts, tan desert boots and tee shirts of various earth-tone colors. All wore their hair short, though not quite military cuts. They'd been talking when Bowman first arrived, but fell silent as he entered, and turned to look at him. Bowman gave them a quick nod and then turned to the man behind the counter.

He was old, probably in his eighties, with unkempt, thin white hair and a two- or three-day growth of white stubble on his chin. He wore a dirty white tee shirt under a pair of overalls. Bowman had come in with his pack in his hand, and he gave the old man a nod as he walked up to the counter and leaned his pack against it. The old man gave Bowman an uncertain smile in greeting, and Bowman turned to look for what he needed in the two aisles of merchandise. Without looking, he could tell that the four men in the back were watching him, and they started talking among themselves again, but now in lower tones, so he couldn't make out what they were saying. Bowman selected a few packages of beef jerky and a handful of energy bars and brought them back to the counter.

While the old man was ringing up his purchases, Bowman wondered how this store could possibly be profitable enough to be worth the trouble, even with the little unofficial cantina in the back. He guessed that it wasn't, at least not anymore, and that the old man lived on his savings, if he had any, or on social security checks. He probably kept it open out of habit, or for something to do with his remaining days.

The four men in the back had apparently come to some conclusion about Bowman. As he was putting his purchases away, one of them said, "How long you been out, soldier?" He appeared to be the oldest of the group, in his mid-thirties, perhaps. He was a little smaller than Bowman, but not much, with dark hair and hazel eyes.

Bowman looked over at the men warily. Four ex-military men in a black SUV didn't add up to some army buddies having a few beers and reliving old times. They looked like colleagues, rather than friends. That suggested private security, but they didn't wear any kind of company identification. He had a bad feeling about this group and had no interest in getting friendly with them, but he didn't want any trouble either. Perhaps the best approach would be a cool politeness.

"About a year," he said, after a moment, and picked up his pack and turned to the door.

"Buy you a beer?" the man said, smiling and gesturing for Bowman to join them.

Bowman turned back. He'd try to walk the line between a friendly attitude, which would probably lead to him spending more time with these men than he cared to, and unfriendly, which could be construed as rude and lead to a confrontation he didn't want.

"No thanks," he said, "I'm walking into town, and I want to be there before dark."

"We'll give you a ride when we're done."

"I'd rather walk," Bowman said, knowing instantly that he'd strayed over the line.

"You don't like us?" This came from one of the others. He was a little smaller than the rest, but he looked meaner and more dangerous. His small, dark eyes were set deep in a thin face, and his mouth was a thin, straight line on his face.

"I don't need any new friends," he said, and started for the door. He didn't want a fight. And if there was going to be violence, he wanted it to happen outside, away from the old man. There wasn't much room to maneuver in the store, and he didn't want the old man caught in the middle of a melee.

Out of the corner of his eye, Bowman saw the smaller man jump up to follow. Here it comes, he thought. The older man grabbed the smaller man's arm to hold him back, but he shook it loose and followed Bowman out the door. The others followed, but just as spectators, it seemed. This was the smaller man's fight, and they were content to watch, at least for now.

Bowman dropped his pack and turned to face his pursuer.

"What the fuck's that s'posed to mean, shithead? You too good to drink with us?"

"I'm just not thirsty. No need to get your panties in a twist."

"I don't like your attitude, jackass."

"What attitude would you prefer? I'm flexible."

That seemed to stump the man, who must have expected a belligerent reply. His eyes narrowed and his jaw tightened. Finally, he said, "You making fun of me?"

Bowman said nothing. There was nothing to say. This man wanted a fight, or a victory of some kind. An apology might do it, if done with an appropriately groveling tone, but Bowman wasn't going to give him that. He didn't want a fight, but he had his pride. He'd wait for the man to make the first move, if he was going to, or talk himself out of it. The other men watched impassively, neither goading their colleague on nor trying to restrain him.

Bowman never went looking for a fight, but it wasn't in his nature to back down. That had landed him in more than a few fights before now, and he'd found that he was good at it. He'd learned hand-to-hand combat in the Army, of course, like everyone else, but he had no special skills or technique. Certainly he was no martial artist. He'd found, however, that he had a natural ability to read his opponent's body language and anticipate his next move, and he was quick enough to take advantage of that knowledge. He hadn't won every fight he'd been in, but he liked his chances now, if it remained one on one.

"I'm talking to you, asshole!"

More often than not, as now, Bowman's opponent was angry and Bowman was not. That was an advantage, because an angry man acts without thinking.

Bowman said nothing.

His silence seemed to push the man over the edge. He

took one quick step towards Bowman and shot his right fist towards Bowman's throat, putting all of his weight behind it. Bowman had been ready for the attack, but was surprised by the ferocity of it. A punch to the throat could crush the windpipe and kill a man by asphyxiation. It was overkill for what was essentially a barroom brawl.

The move was fast, but Bowman was just able to twist back and away in time to avoid the blow, moving his right foot back as he did so. The other man's momentum had carried his twisted torso too far to his left, and too low. He'd clearly counted on landing his first blow. Bowman brought his two hands, clenched together to form one large fist, down on the back of the man's head, even as he brought his right leg forward and drove his knee up into the man's face. His clenched hands made contact before his knee could make it to the fight, knocking the man's head down into the upcoming knee, which made contact a fraction of a second later. There was a thump, thump, followed by a flop as the man collapsed in the dust. The fight had lasted no more than two seconds.

Bowman stepped back quickly and prepared to meet any attack from the other men, but none came. Their faces were impassive, or perhaps he detected suppressed smiles. Certainly, they showed no inclination to avenge their fallen comrade. Bowman was relieved. He had no illusions about his chances in a fight against three such men.

After a few seconds, two of them helped the man up. He was now groaning wetly, blood pouring from his nose and mouth. The older man, the one who had first spoken to him, gave Bowman an appraising look.

"I guess he asked for that," he said. "He's a bit of a hot head." After a short pause, he continued, "I offered to buy you a drink because I wanted to talk to you about something. You look like you could use a job, and we can always use men like you."

By 'men like you,' Bowman presumed he meant ex-military, like them. He'd already decided that he didn't want anything to do with these men, especially now that he'd made an enemy of one of them.

"I'm not much of a joiner," he said.

"Fair enough," the man said after a moment. "They call me Gordon. If you change your mind you can reach us through old Gabe in there." He motioned with his head towards the store. "We come here from time to time. He can take a message for us."

By this time, the others had gotten the bleeding man into the black SUV, and Gordon climbed into the driver's seat. They drove off, heading away from Tierra Roja. Bowman watched them until they were out of sight, then shouldered his pack and started to walk towards town.

That was only yesterday, or the day before yesterday if it was after midnight, and now he was lying in a jail cell, suspected of murder. Was there a connection between those men and the murder, or his arrest? If so, Bowman couldn't imagine what it might be.

Morning came and Bowman hadn't arrived at any answers when the face of Sheriff Cane appeared in the door window. After seeing where Bowman was sitting on his cot, Cane opened the door and tossed in Bowman's backpack, his boots and a bundle of his clothes.

"You're free to go, son," he said. "Change out of your government clothes and knock on the door when you're dressed." He then closed the door and stepped away from the window to give Bowman some privacy.

Bowman looked through his pack and the bundle of clothes. Nothing was in its usual place, but everything seemed to be there, except his knife. In certain parts of the country there were laws against carrying a knife like his, and he didn't know what the law was in Bronco County, New Mexico. He'd hate to lose the knife, but there wouldn't be much he could do about it if they decided to confiscate it.

He assumed that they'd examined everything for traces

of blood or any other evidence, and that they'd done the same to his room at the motel. They hadn't found anything, of course.

He shed his orange jumpsuit and pulled on his own clothes. He left the jumpsuit and slippers on the floor, pulled his pack over his shoulder and knocked on the door.

Sheriff Cane opened the door and led him back through the station house. Mrs. Flores was at her desk. She looked flustered, and avoided his gaze. He thought of saying 'Good morning,' but didn't. It would only embarrass her, and there was no need for that. Outside of his office, Cane pointed to a pot of coffee and a box of donuts.

"Why don't you have a cup of coffee and a couple of donuts? I need to make some calls, and then I'll give you a ride out of town."

Bowman bristled. He'd been thinking of getting a proper breakfast, finding a laundromat and a barber, and maybe buying some essentials before going on. He didn't know how soon he would have another chance.

"I thought you said I was free to go."

Cane had started to go into his office, but stopped and turned back to Bowman. "Now you listen to me, son. The DA thinks we don't have enough evidence to hold you, and Detective Carrillo doesn't think you're the man we want. I don't either. But this town is pretty tore up over these murders, and lots of folks around here aren't so sure you aren't the murderer. In fact, we had a concerned citizen come by yesterday, with blood in his eyes. You may have heard him."

"I did, and he sure did sound concerned."

"And he's not the only one, although certainly the most concerned. 'Most everyone in the County owns a gun, and in this part of the country there's a long history of self-help in matters of justice. I reckon it's a good idea for you to be out of town and on your way as soon as convenient."

This all rang true to Bowman, and he relaxed. The Sheriff wasn't trying to run him out of town, or at least not for the wrong reasons.

"Sure, Sheriff, I see your point. But what about my knife?"

"I'll give that back to you when I drop you off outside of town. Just give me a couple of minutes and I'll be ready to go," he said, and walked into his office and closed the door.

Bowman poured himself a cup of coffee. There was non-dairy creamer and sugar on the table, but he didn't take any. He liked coffee, and didn't see the point of diluting the flavor, if it was good coffee. This coffee was good, and so were the donuts. Trust cops to have good donuts, he thought, and smiled to himself.

Bowman had eaten two donuts and finished his coffee when Cane emerged from his office. He'd put his hat on and was carrying Bowman's knife in its sheath.

"Which way you wanna go?"

"West," said Bowman, "the way I was going when you arrested me."

"If you're looking for an apology, son, you're in for a disappointment. I'm sorry you were inconvenienced, but I don't think we did anything wrong in bringing you in. Given the same circumstances, I'd do it again."

Bowman felt chastened. He realized that his tone had been reproachful, and that the reproach was not deserved.

"No hard feelings on my end, Sheriff. I only meant that I want to keep going west."

"There isn't much in that direction but desert for a lot of miles. And not much traffic. It may be hard to catch a ride. You sure you don't want me to take you out to the bus stop on the highway?"

"No, I'll take my chances," Bowman said.

"Suit yourself."

Cane led the way out to the parking lot. It was good to be in the open air again. When they got to the police cruiser, Cane climbed into the driver's seat. Bowman opened the rear door, tossed in his pack and started to climb in after it.

"Jump in the front, son. You aren't under arrest. Just don't touch anything."

Bowman got in next to Cane. He was accustomed to riding in the back when he was being run out of town, and he appreciated the gesture. On the front seat, between Cane and Bowman, was a sack lunch, a bottle of water and Bowman's knife. Cane pulled out of the parking lot, and they drove in silence for a while.

After a few minutes, Bowman said, "Sheriff, I got the impression that Detective Carrillo thought that the murders were committed by a hired killer, to send some kind of message. Why would anyone want to kill a young woman and a child? Were they witnesses to a crime or something?"

Cane seemed surprised by the question, and looked inquiringly at Bowman. He took some time to reply, but apparently resolved whatever questions were going through his mind, for when he did, he said, "Mary Walker's husband, and little Emma's father, is a man named Bill Walker. Bill is a DEA agent who lives here in town, and he was the concerned citizen I mentioned. He's been bringing a lot of hurt to some of the drug traffickers in the area, and about a month ago he busted up a major deal. DEA arrested some major players, and confiscated enough heroin to keep the whole Southwest stoned for a week. I heard tell the street value was north of ten million dollars. That pissed off some very dangerous people, people who'd kill innocent women and children by the dozen if it would discourage that sort of DEA activity. Call it revenge, call it sending a message. Either way, message received."

Bowman shuddered. Would someone really do that? Even drug dealers?

"Carrillo mentioned someone named El Chato. Is he

one of those dangerous people?"

"One of the worst. That's a nickname, of course. Means flat face, or chubby face, or something like that. Don't know if anyone knows his real name. I know I don't." He paused, then added, "Not your concern now, though. Why so curious?"

Bowman thought for a moment, looking out the side window as they passed the last few houses on the edge of town. Then he turned to Cane and said, "I'm not sure. I guess I feel connected to all this now. Hard to just put it out of my mind after having my nose rubbed in it like this." And it reminds me of something I've been trying to forget, Bowman thought.

"Yeah, I guess I know what you mean. But there'll be no shortage of people focusing on this problem. Law enforcement can't let somebody get away with something like this. Cops get killed in the line of duty from time to time, and the response is always massive if the perp's not caught or killed on the scene. But this, killing a man's family, takes it to a whole 'nother level. There's a ton of bricks waiting to fall on El Chato and his people. But he's a slippery son of a bitch. We think he operates out of this general area, but we haven't been able to find him. We will, though, and when we do it won't be pretty."

They drove in silence for a while. Bowman could see that Cane's mind was working, and his face took on a hard, determined look, like it had been carved out of oak. I would not want this man for an enemy, he thought. After a bit, Cane continued, "These Mexican drug cartels are starting to move north of the border, and bringing their ways of doing business with them. I hear that this sort of thing, targeting a lawman's family, happens in Mexico from time to time. If we let them get away with that up here even once it'll become a regular thing, and I don't want to live in that kind of world."

"But why now, Sheriff? What's changed?"

Cane said nothing for a long while, apparently thinking,

and Bowman began to think that he wasn't going to answer the question. He noticed that the houses on the side of the road were now widely separated, and decidedly more down-market, one-story cinder block houses with rusty pickup trucks parked outside, big dogs chained in dusty front yards and nothing but desert as far as the eye could see for back yards. Bowman realized the Cane was not so much a small-town cop as a territorial lawman. There was a lot of space out here.

Finally, Cane said, "I'm not sure. I think they're following the profits of the heroin trade. Only a few years ago we'd hardly ever see heroin in this county. We've had crystal meth for a long time, and that's bad enough. But heroin is relatively new in these parts. It was the sort of thing rock stars did, or in the big city slums. Now it's common around here, almost. And crystal meth has been a problem mostly for those on the margins, if you know what I mean. Folks whose lives weren't working out too well even before they started on the meth. These heroin addicts, on the other hand, are middle-class kids, from good families. Son of a good friend of mine died of an overdose a couple of years ago."

"Why do you think that is? Why is heroin so popular, all of a sudden?"

"I think it started with prescription pain killers. I don't know if they're more effective than they used to be, or are just prescribed more. Anyway, some high school football player breaks a collar bone or something and they give him a prescription for one of those opium-based pain killers. He likes the way it makes him feel, and when his prescription runs out, he goes looking for more on the street. If he can't find the pills, or can't afford them, he tries heroin. It's not hard to find these days, and it's relatively cheap. That's kind of what happened to this kid I mentioned."

That overdose must have shaken him, thought Bowman. It was the second time he'd mentioned it.

"Because the Mexican cartels are moving north?"

"I don't know which came first, the supply or the demand, but making it easier to get sure isn't helping any."

"Is heroin worse than crystal meth, I mean apart from who is using it?"

"Well, heroin will kill you quicker, if you OD. But meth is more certain to ruin you in the long haul. It doesn't really matter which is worse, though, because it's not like heroin is replacing meth. The heroin users are not ex meth heads, if there is such a thing. Heroin is a whole new problem, dropped on top of our meth problem."

They were now a couple of miles past the edge of town, and Cane pulled over. There were no houses in sight, just desert and road. The morning was still fresh and cool, but Bowman knew that wouldn't last long. He got out of the car, gathered his pack from the back seat and walked up to the driver's side window, which Cane had rolled down.

"Here's your tool, son, and a bottle of water and something to eat. There's a peanut butter and jelly sandwich and an apple in there. It should keep for a while."

"Thank you, Sheriff," said Bowman. Cane was a considerate man. He hadn't seen much of this kind of treatment lately.

"Good luck, son. I'm glad I didn't shoot you."

"You looked like you wanted to."

"I did," Cane said, and pulled the cruiser around in a U turn and headed back towards town.

CHAPTER 6

"Do you think we did the right thing, Ernesto, letting that Bowman guy go?" Paine said, and took a sip of his coffee.

He and Carrillo were back at the headquarters of the New Mexico State Police Special Investigations Bureau, in Clovis, where they shared an office. Their desks were pushed together so that they faced each other. Paine had his chair pulled out, his jacket draped over the back it, and his legs extended to the side. His left arm rested on his desk and he held his coffee in his right hand. Carrillo was looking through some papers on his desk, his jacket on and his tie neatly knotted. Paine didn't think he'd ever seen Carrillo in his shirt sleeves.

"I do, Terrance," said Carrillo, looking up from his papers and taking off his reading glasses.

Carrillo was the only person on Earth who called him Terrance, rather than Terry, Paine thought as he shooed away a fly that had taken an unhealthy interest in his coffee, or more likely the milk and sugar in it. He'd condescend to use Paine's first name, and to be addressed by his own first name, because to do otherwise would give offense, and a gentleman didn't give offense if he could avoid it. But he couldn't bring himself to use the name Terry. The funny thing was, Paine liked the name Terrance, and wished he could get others to call him that instead of Terry. But suggesting that would come off as pretentious at this point.

Carrillo continued, "We have no evidence of his guilt, and what evidence we do have points elsewhere. In addition to all this, my intuition tells me that he is not the murderer."

Paine knew better than to scoff at Carrillo's intuition. It had been proved accurate often enough. "Yeah, I hear you, but he was hiding something. He wouldn't tell us why he went to see the Army psychologist in Iraq."

Carrillo took a cloth from a jacket pocket and started polishing his glasses. "We are all hiding something, Terrance. Something was troubling Mr. Bowman in Iraq, something that troubles him still, I think. But that is no sin. The worst of men are those who are never troubled. I think it is significant that he did not lie to us. He could have told us anything, but he simply refused to discuss it."

Paine decided that the fly would have to die if he wanted to finish his coffee in peace. He swung his legs around under his desk, put his coffee cup down and picked up his folded copy of The Clovis News Journal. Then he waited for his enemy to land on a surface within reach.

"We would've known if he was bullshitting us," Paine said, and immediately regretted using the crude term. Anyone who spent any time with Carrillo learned to avoid vulgarity in his presence, unless you were playing bad cop, of course. He'd never object, exactly, but he would get a pained look on his face, like the one he had now. It made you feel ashamed, like a little boy caught wetting the bed. Vulgarity wasn't uncommon among cops, and anyone else who was offended by it would've been mocked mercilessly. But no one mocked Carrillo, and everyone tried to conform to his notions of decorum when in his presence. He pulled it off, Paine thought, because it was clear to all who knew him that Carrillo was the real deal, and not acting a part. He was an eighteenth-century gentleman who had wandered into the twenty-first century. He wasn't unfriendly, but he discouraged familiarity. They'd been working together for five years, and Paine still knew very little about Carrillo's private life.

"Yes, perhaps we would have known if he were – lying – to us," said Carrillo, "but we could not have disproved anything he chose to say about it. I think a guilty man would have lied, if he felt he could not, for some reason, tell the truth. But that is based on nothing more than my intuition. Intuition can be a valuable guide, but our decisions must be based upon the facts."

The fly declined to land anywhere other than on or in his coffee cup, where he couldn't swat it without risking spilling his coffee, so after shooing it away a few more times Paine decided to lay a trap. He took the plastic stirring stick out of the coffee cup and covered the cup with his day planner, then set the stick and its attached drop of coffee on the middle of his gray metal government desk. Carrillo watched with apparent amusement, but made no comment.

"So let's go over the facts, again, Ernesto. What have we got?"

"Very little, as you know, Terrance. To begin with, there are the footprints in and around the backyard. Some of them are from boots, perhaps combat boots."

"Like the ones Bowman was wearing."

"Yes, but some of them looked like they were made a day or more prior to the murder, before Mr. Bowman arrived in Tierra Roja. I believe the killer was observing the house for a few nights before the night of the murders. No, Mr. Bowman did not leave those footprints."

"Whoever it was probably poisoned that dog too."

"Very likely. And that was several days before the murder."

"But how do we know that Bowman didn't arrive earlier than he said? All we have is his word for it."

"Would it make sense for him to hide out in the area for several days, without being seen, and then check into a motel the night of the murder? I think not. And the footprints did not have the same tread pattern as Mr. Bowman's boots, and were a smaller size."

The fly had realized by now that its access to the coffee in the cup was effectively blocked, and it was circling the drop of coffee on Paine's desk, no doubt tempted but suspicious.

"Yeah, you're right, of course. I guess I'm just frustrated. I thought we had our man."

"So did I, but I now wish that I could help him somehow. He carries a burden of some kind, and is quite alone in the world, Terrance. Consider what that means. If he were to die in the street, there would be no one to claim his body, no one to feel the loss, no one to care." Carrillo paused, seemingly lost in thought, and then continued, "But Mr. Bowman must make his way as best he can, and we must persevere in our search for the truth. Did you notice that some of the footprints were – muted, or obscured somehow?"

"Yes, I did. A second perp, you think?"

"Perhaps, but I think it is more likely that the killer was wearing something over his boots, some of the time. Not to obscure his footprints, or he would have worn them all of the time. I think he put on some kind of protective covering before entering the house, over his boots or perhaps over his entire body, to avoid contaminating his clothes or leaving fiber evidence at the scene. Certainly, we did not find any such evidence, apart from what we found in the kitchen sink trap."

"And most of that was from the victims. All but that one strand of hair."

"Exactly, Terrance. That one strand of hair does not match the victims or Mr. Walker, nor does it match the samples of Mr. Bowman's hair we recovered from his hat. I think it is very likely that the owner of that strand of hair is the murderer. Until we have another sample of the killer's hair, all that we can deduce from it is that we are looking for a Caucasian with dark brown hair. I am afraid it does not narrow down the field much, but if we find the killer that strand of hair could help to positively identify him."

At last, the fly overcame its suspicion and landed by the drop of coffee. Paine slowly began to raise the newspaper, being careful not to make any sudden movement or create any wind.

"And you think the killer has something against women?"

"Yes, due to the – unusual nature of some of the wounds."

"Yeah, I know what you mean." Paine did know what Carrillo meant, and didn't like to think about it. The Clovis News Journal came down with all the force of Paine's outrage behind it, making a loud slapping sound and putting an end to the fly's short career. This was some sick bastard they were after. And his own intuition, such as it was, agreed with Carrillo's. Bowman didn't seem like the kind of guy that could do that. "I guess I agree with you about Bowman, but the murder weapon could've been something like that knife of his, right?"

Paine retrieved his coffee cup from under his day planner, turned to the side again to stretch his legs, and took a sip. It had gone cold.

"Yes, a heavy blade, and wielded with great strength. Almost certainly a man, for that and – the other reasons we mentioned."

"And no fingerprints. We don't have much to go on, do we?"

"Our most promising lead, I think, is the motive. If we are correct in our surmise that the motive for the killings was revenge for Agent Walker's recent disruption of El

Chato's business, then we will find our killer when we find El Chato."

"And how do we do that, Ernesto?"

"That I do not know. But I have been reading this file on what the Drug Enforcement Administration has learned about him, and perhaps that will yield some ideas. Would you like to see it when I have finished?"

"Yes, please. And one other thing."

"What is that?"

"Why do I always have to be the bad cop?"

Carrillo smiled, and Paine laughed. They both knew the answer.

"I think, Terrance, that you would make an excellent good cop, but I fear that I would not make a convincing bad cop."

CHAPTER 7

Bowman had saved the sandwich and apple all day, and ate them while he waited for the sun to set and the full moon to rise. The bag had also contained a bite-sized chocolate bar, which he ate as well. Bowman couldn't picture Sheriff Cane packing a candy bar with his lunch. He seemed like more of a bacon and beans man. He guessed that the Sheriff's wife had packed his lunch for him, and added the candy bar as a little sign of affection.

Sheriff Cane was a lucky man.

He'd walked for a few hours, till about noon, judging by the sun. The battery in his watch had died a while back, and he hadn't felt the need to replace it. He had no trains to catch or appointments to keep. A few cars had passed, but none stopped for him. The road had started to angle towards the north, and Bowman had decided to continue west, which meant cutting across country. He had no particular reason for going west, rather than north or any other direction, but he'd decided he was going west, and had made a point of it with Cane. So he would go west.

The decision to head off the road was made on a whim, but he knew the dangers. This was desert country. It would be easy to get lost, easy to die of thirst or heat stroke. He'd need to draw on his desert survival training, but a bit of wandering in the wilderness appealed to him. It would be good for the soul, and he felt in need of it. Ishmael had gone to sea to soothe his soul. Bowman would go for a walk in the desert to soothe his.

So he'd found a patch of mesquite trees that provided some shade and had rested during the heat of the day. He read some more of Moby Dick, and dozed off from time to time, but mostly he took in the desert around him.

Groups of buzzards rode the thermals, turning in slow circles as they searched the landscape for their next meal. A road runner trotted by less than ten yards away, and he half expected to see that hapless coyote right behind it. The bird wasn't as colorful as the one in the cartoon, but it was handsome, with a sense of style. Some kind of lizard darted in from his right and stopped dead just in front of him. Its camouflage coloring was so effective that he might not have noticed it if he hadn't seen it running. It remained completely motionless for several minutes, and then darted off again. It was like he was playing a game of freeze tag; you're either running at full speed or not moving at all.

There was a lot to see almost anywhere you were, if you had patience and took the time to look for it. He appreciated the beauty of nature now in a way that he hadn't before the wars. Was it just maturity, or had his long dance with death somehow sharpened his taste for life? He liked to think that some good had come with the bad.

The moon was full, which would allow him to travel quickly and safely, he hoped. He didn't know how far he would need to go before he came to another road or settlement, but he didn't think it would be more than two or three days. This was New Mexico, not the Sahara.

The moon was up in the east even as the sun set in the west, and Bowman got up and started out, heading towards the setting sun. He had a compass, but didn't think he would need it tonight. He'd start out with the moon behind him, but would be heading towards it come dawn, as the moon followed the sun from east to west. Or nearly so. On a solar equinox, when the day and night were of equal length, the full moon, like the sun, would rise due east and set due west. But in late June, the sun would rise a bit north of east and set a bit north of west, while the full moon would follow the path of the mid-winter sun. It would rise a bit south of east and set a bit south of west. He'd adjust for that, but didn't need to be precise. As long as he continued more or less in the same direction, and didn't end up going in circles, he would emerge from the desert eventually.

The night was cool, a perfect temperature for hiking over the rough terrain of gravelly soil and limestone outcroppings. The landscape was cut from time to time by arroyos and dry creek beds, and various kinds of cacti, yucca and sagebrush were scattered about. Bowman thought it looked starkly beautiful in the moonlight, but knew that it would not have the same charm in the heat of the day. By dawn, or shortly after, he would need to find a shady place to spend the day. And he would need to keep an eye out for possible water sources. He still had a little water left in his bottle, but it would be gone well before dawn, and his canteen was empty. If he'd thought that he'd be crossing a desert that day, he would've filled it before he left town. He should've done it anyway. Lesson learned. Sheriff Cane's lunch hadn't satisfied his hunger, but he tried to ignore that. He still had his beef jerky and energy bars, but food required water to digest. He could go for days without food before it would start to impair his effectiveness, so he decided to put food out of his mind, if he could, until he had a secure water supply.

As he walked, Bowman let his mind wander. He thought about growing up in rural Montana, and about joining the Army as a way of getting out of there and seeing something different. It was different, all right. He couldn't remember anymore what he'd expected, but it wasn't what he got. He thought about his parents, and felt a pang of sorrow and remorse. He was all they'd had, after Bridget left, and he had gone away himself. They'd been supportive when he announced that he was joining the Army, but he knew that they missed him and worried about him. It was kind of ironic; he had survived his military service, but they had not.

And where was Bridget? Was she happy? He was certain that she was alive, although he couldn't say why. He'd idolized his big sister when he was little, and would tag along with her whenever she would let him. She and her friends had doted on him, and made him feel special, like when they would invite him to their tea parties. As they got older, they'd gone their separate ways, as befit their different ages and sexes, but they'd remained close. Or at least he had thought so. He never understood why she ran away, except that it had to do with some stupid argument with Mom and Dad. His parents had hired a private investigator to try to find her, an expense they couldn't afford, but he had failed to find anything. After all these years, it wouldn't be any easier. He knew his search for her was futile, but he had to try. And what else did he have to do?

He kept walking. He was making good time, and there would be plenty of time to rest during the heat of the day tomorrow. Sometime deep in the night he saw a coyote trotting along a ridge about a hundred yards away, silhouetted against the sky, its nose and tail low to the ground. It was moving purposefully, and seemed to be on the trail of something, or at least to know where it was going, and why. Bowman envied him for that.

The coyote reminded him of Reggie. Poor Reggie, he thought, I should have been nicer to him.

Reggie had been his first dog, or rather Bridget's dog. He had died when Bowman was a small child, and he could only remember the last few months of Reggie's life.

Reggie's death had affected him more than the deaths of any of his other dogs, even more than the deaths of some people he had known, and that was because he felt responsible for Reggie's death.

He knew why he felt responsible, and he knew that he shouldn't, but you don't get to choose what you feel. He had wanted a new puppy, and his father had said that he couldn't have one until Reggie was no longer with them. So he had wished for Reggie to be gone, and then he had died. In his childish mind, that wish had been the cause of Reggie's death and the pain it had caused, particularly for Bridget, who had loved him.

He knew now, of course, that a wish cannot kill. He knew now that a child cannot be expected to understand the finality of death. He knew now that he should not feel guilty.

But he did.

About an hour after spotting the coyote, he heard some shuffling and grunting in the underbrush that sounded like pigs. Based upon what he'd read in his Army desert survival manual, he guessed it was a group of peccaries. Sound travels well in the clear desert night, and he couldn't judge how close they were. He couldn't smell them – they are sometimes called stink pigs, though not actually pigs – so he thought he wasn't likely to stumble upon them. If startled, they could do a great deal of damage with their tusks, and almost any injury could be life-threatening this far from help. The presence of peccaries suggested that water was nearby, as they tended to stick close to a source of it, so he made a mental note to keep an eye out for animal trails.

Not long after hearing the peccaries, he did spot what looked like a trail, and followed it a short distance until it joined another trail. The two trails forked, rather than converged, so he realized that he was going the wrong way. Just as rivers and their tributaries will converge on their way to the sea, animal trails will converge upon any common destination, such as a water source. As he followed the trail in the opposite direction, other trails joined it from time to time, all going the same way. In about twenty minutes he came to a jumble of large boulders, in the middle of which, in a place that would be well shaded in daylight, was a small pool of water in an indentation in the rock. This natural cistern was fed by a spring that trickled water down the rocks to be collected in the pool. He drank what remained of his bottled water and filled the bottle and his canteen from the pool. The water wasn't deep enough to fully submerge either, but he was able to fill both by using a cupped hand. He dropped an iodine pill in each, screwed on the tops and put them in his pack. It would take about thirty minutes for the iodine to dissolve completely and purify the water, so he shouldered his pack and continued towards the west.

The terrain was gradually becoming rougher and hillier. He saw no more wildlife, but he knew there would be plenty of it about him, watching him. He felt very small, lost in the vastness of the landscape. The feeling was a bit scary, but also exhilarating. Was this something like how it felt to be at sea, surrounded by water as far as the eye could see? He didn't know, but he knew that this is what he'd come for. Out here, he could imagine that he was the last man on earth, or the first, with no past and no future. There was nothing to remember, or forget, and nothing to apprehend, or dread. He didn't need to think about where he should go, or what he should do. There was only the present, and the sights, sounds, smells and sensations of this time and place.

Shortly before dawn, just as the sky was getting noticeably lighter in the east, he topped a small rise overlooking a group of buildings that looked like an abandoned mining camp. The camp was surrounded by a ring of small hills and rock outcroppings. The ring was broken by gaps here and there, but the higher ground overlapped in such a way that one would need to be within the ring, or on the higher ground around it, as he was, to see the camp in the middle. If his path had taken him even a few hundred yards to his left or right, he never would've seen it. As far as Bowman could see, there were no roads or utility lines leading into the camp. It looked old, decrepit and abandoned. This would be a good place to hole up and rest during the day, out of the sun. Perhaps he would even find a well, some canned food or something else useful.

This thought cheered him considerably, and he started down the slope towards the camp.

Then, suddenly, he stopped, sensing that something was wrong. He didn't understand at first what troubled him, but he trusted his instincts. Instinct wasn't a magical sixth sense, but simply your subconscious mind sensing or understanding something that your conscious mind hadn't yet picked up on. It was wise to heed it. There was no sign of life or movement in the camp, but something was wrong. After a few moments, it registered with his conscious mind, a low hum or rumble, just barely audible. A generator.

Normally, a generator would be much noisier, especially in the desert quiet. This generator was muffled, somehow, perhaps inside a building or sound-proofed enclosure. Were there lights? He hadn't seen any, but now he looked more closely. At a few windows or doors, it was hard to tell which from this distance and in the darkness of pre-dawn, he could just make out slivers of light, as if black-out shades were in place but not completely effective at some of the edges. Someone was in the camp, someone who didn't want to be found.

Or maybe he was imagining things. He decided to wait for daylight, to get a better look at the camp, before deciding whether to go down into the camp or skirt around it.

Scouting his hilltop, he found a spot among some boulders and vegetation that promised shade, concealment and a good view of the camp. He examined his hiding place carefully for scorpions, snakes and other creatures and, seeing none, crawled in and waited for the sun.

CHAPTER 8

The sellers had chosen an isolated barn, and the middle of the night, for the transaction. The buyers' group travelled in two black SUVs, the Mexicans in the front one and the Americans in the other. Gordon was driving the Americans. Next to him was Ford, and Sanborn was in the back. Hawk wasn't with them this time, because of his face. It had been two days, and it looked better now than it had – it was no longer visibly swollen – but it was still a purplish-yellow color. El Chato and Gordon had decided that the condition of Hawk's face would not reflect well on them, so they left him back at base with Bravo Squad.

As soon as they'd gotten back from old Gabe's cantina a couple of days previously, Gordon had told El Chato how Hawk had acquired his injuries. El Chato had then spoken to Hawk alone, and had sent him off on some errand or other, as he often did. Gordon didn't know what kind of errands, and didn't want to know.

The man at the cantina had intrigued him. Maybe they should swing by Tierra Roja again and see if they could spot him. He might be more amenable to Gordon's offer, after he'd had some time to think about it.

When they arrived at the site, there were two other

black SUVs parked in front of the barn, to the left of a large, open door. They parked on the other side of the door. The sellers' SUVs were empty, and a light shone from the barn's open door. There was no sound, other than the buzz of insects. Gordon, Ford and Sanborn exited their vehicle first, and formed a semi-circle around El Chato's SUV, their rifles in hand and facing away from the car. Gordon was in the center of the three, with Ford's long and lanky frame to his right and Sanborn's short, squat frame to his left. Gordon was like an average of the other two, a bit over average height and solidly built.

None of the Americans in his security team used their real names, and Gordon liked to speculate about how each of them had picked his nom de guerre. He knew that his speculations were probably wrong. Certainly none of them could ever guess how he had chosen his own. Maybe Ford was partial to that brand of truck, or maybe he chose it for its ordinariness, like Jones or Smith. It was anonymous and unmemorable. That was probably it. Ford had something going on between his ears, unlike Sanborn. Sanborn was easy enough to work with, but not the sharpest tool in the shed. That was probably his real name.

Only when the American security was in place did El Chato, Esteban, Paco and Pedro emerge from their SUV. All of the Mexicans carried side arms, but only Esteban carried a rifle. Pedro carried a black vinyl bag containing the cash.

El Chato was named for his face, which looked like it could have been lifted from a bas relief carving on an Aztec temple. It was square and flat, with a wide nose and high cheekbones. And he was much darker than his Mexican companions. Esteban, his right hand man, was taller and thinner, with an intense gaze that reminded Gordon of Hawk's. Gordon didn't like any of the Mexicans, but considered Esteban to be the worst of them. Even worse than El Chato.

Once they were all assembled, El Chato led the way through the open door, his group close by his side. He was the shortest of them all, but there was no mistaking who was boss. He carried himself with an assurance and authority that was unmistakable. Gordon and the other Americans followed a few paces behind, keeping as spread out as they could.

A single bulb hung from the rafters in the middle of the barn, creating a circle of light that didn't quite fill the building. The sellers stood a bit past the middle of the circle, four Hispanic men dressed in black. All wore side arms, but none carried rifles. One of the men carried a silver metal suitcase containing, Gordon knew, the drugs. Gordon couldn't see the other security team, his counterparts, but knew they were there, in the shadows. He also knew that they were at least as well armed as his men and knew their business. El Chato and his Mexicans walked to the center of the circle, but Gordon stayed just outside the light, and whispered to Sanborn and Ford to do the same. He suspected that they had him flanked, and maybe even encircled, but there was nothing he could do about that.

Pedro handed the bag of cash to one of the men in black, who opened it, counted the bundles and examined one of them closely. He nodded, and another man in black handed El Chato the silver suitcase. El Chato opened it and quickly scanned the contents, then closed it and nodded. Gordon suspected that the scrutiny had been for form's sake; if these men wanted to cheat El Chato, they could and would, and there wasn't much he could do about it, other than to stop doing business with them. And if these men ever decided that they no longer wished to do business with El Chato, there would not be much to stop them from killing him and all his people and keeping everything. Gordon's job was to make that option, if not difficult, at least costly and dangerous. He had no illusions about how it would end for him and the other Americans if things went sour, and he was on edge. But for now it was a mutually beneficial relationship.

If El Chato was nervous, he didn't show it. Nor did Esteban, but Paco and Pedro were shuffling their feet more than was strictly necessary.

Once the transaction was completed, El Chato exchanged a few muttered words with his counterpart, nodded, and then strode calmly back through the door, followed by Paco, Pedro and Esteban. Gordon had to admire the man's nerve. He let them pass through his line of men, and then they followed, once again keeping as widely spaced as possible. After El Chato and his Mexicans were in their SUV, Gordon and his men climbed into theirs and the two SUVs drove away from the barn. Only after they were moving did Gordon feel the tension start to drain from his neck and shoulders.

"I didn't like that set up," said Ford, wiping his forehead with his shirt sleeve. "I didn't see any of them. They could've been anywhere, and it wouldn't surprise me if they had night vision goggles."

"Yes," said Gordon, "that was a bit uncomfortable."

Sanborn said nothing, but nodded in agreement.

It was dawn by the time they got back to base. After breakfast, Gordon's men, Alpha Squad, caught a few hours of sleep and left Bravo Squad on duty.

After a few hours of sleep, Alpha Squad took over from Bravo Squad, but there wasn't much to do. They just had to be awake and armed, ready to respond to any threats that might arise, and Gordon didn't think that they were likely to face any threats out here in the middle of nowhere. Occasionally one of them would go outside and walk up and down the central avenue a couple of times, and scan the surrounding desert. But mostly Gordon, Ford and Sanborn passed the time talking, reading magazines or playing cards. Hawk kept to himself, as always.

The afternoon passed into evening, and they pulled

down the shades and turned the lights on. Samson, from Bravo Squad, joined them for a game of five card draw poker. Samson was built like a weight lifter, and seemed excessively proud of his physique. He walked with that kind of swagger. That and his dark hair and complexion explained the name, thought Gordon. Perhaps he was fleeing some Delilah with a sharp pair of scissors.

The ante was five dollars apiece, to start the pot out at twenty. Gordon sat to the left of Ford, who was dealing, and was dealt a pair of jacks, a king, a seven and a five. He led the betting with ten dollars, the limit. Samson and Sanborn saw his ten, but Ford saw it and raised it five dollars. Gordon's hand wasn't promising, but he thought that Ford had a tendency to bluff, so he saw the five dollars but didn't raise it. Samson saw the five as well, and Sanborn folded.

"Too rich for my blood," he said.

That brought the pot to seventy-five dollars. Gordon thought of discarding three cards, all but the pair of jacks, and drawing three more. It was probably the best move, statistically, but it would betray a weak hand. So he held on to the king and drew two cards, a six and a king. That made two pair, which should be good enough. Samson drew three cards, which increased Gordon's confidence, but Ford stood pat, and drew none.

"I'm good," he said with a smirk.

That meant that he was either bluffing or had a better hand than Gordon. Any hand that required all five cards was better than two pair. Gordon thought he could read Sanborn and Samson, but not Ford. Those waters ran deep.

"You're full of shit, Ford," said Gordon, trying to show more confidence than he felt. "You've got nothing. I bet ten."

"I don't know about Ford, but I know I've got nothing. I'm out," said Samson, throwing down his cards with a look of disgust.

"I'll see your ten and raise you ten," said Ford. "You're already in for forty bucks, Gordon. You're not gonna let me walk away with the pot just to avoid risking another ten are you?"

And that was the truth, although he still suspected that Ford's taunting was just part of a bluff.

"No I am not, my friend," said Gordon, sliding another ten-dollar bill into the pot. "Now read 'em and weep."

But just as Gordon was about to show what he hoped was a winning hand of two pair, kings and jacks, the lights went out.

CHAPTER 9

Bowman brushed away the ever-present gnats and took a sip of water. It was about noon, and he'd been watching the camp since dawn. He'd quickly confirmed that the camp was occupied, and by heavily armed men. Shortly after dawn, he'd seen two black SUVs drive through a gap in the hills and into the camp. Both had heavy-duty suspensions and off-road tires. They'd driven into one of the buildings, then come back out on foot and walked to other buildings. All seven were armed. Four of the seven carried rifles of some kind, and all wore pistols on their hips. One carried what looked like a submachine gun; the others looked like M4 assault rifles. None wore any kind of uniform, but three of them, the ones carrying the M4s, were dressed like the four men he'd encountered at the little cantina two days ago. At this distance, he couldn't tell for sure if any of them were the same men, but it seemed likely. The other four men, including the guy with the submachine gun, wore white shirts outside of dark pants, and looked Hispanic. Those in the white shirts had walked to one of the buildings, and the other men had walked to another.

The area enclosed by the higher ground looked to be

only a few hundred yards wide, and the cluster of camp buildings covered about one quarter of that area. The camp consisted of six main buildings and a small shed. The shed seemed to be where the generator was, since cables ran from the shed to three of the main buildings, along the ground and mostly covered with sand. The other three buildings, the ones not connected to the generator, looked long abandoned, with gaping windows and doors hanging on one or two hinges, or missing entirely. Their roofs had caved in here and there. The three buildings connected to the generator looked similar, at first glance. Looking carefully, he could see that the gray, weathered wood and sagging roofs of these three were just camouflage laid over new construction. From the air, especially, all of this would look like the abandoned mining camp that it had once been, patches of gray on a sandy brown background. Bowman guessed that the new buildings were constructed on the spot where old, abandoned buildings had stood, and that parts of those old buildings had been used as the camouflage. Even someone familiar with this old camp and flying over it would see the same number of buildings, in the same places. In the side of the hill opposite Bowman, on the other side of the camp, was a mine shaft. It was boarded up and looked long abandoned.

From time to time, one or more of them would walk from one of the buildings to another, or do some cursory patrolling of the area. Some of them were from the group of seven that had arrived that morning, but at least three were not. So there were at least ten armed men in the camp. In addition to the weapons he'd seen earlier, one of them carried some kind of scoped long gun. Bowman had decided to skirt the camp as soon as it got dark, and continue west. When he reached civilization, he would call Sheriff Cane and report what he'd seen. Cane could take it from there. It was clear that these people were up to no good. Drug traffickers, probably. Maybe they were El

Chato's people. He hoped so. It should be easy enough to send a small army of law enforcement officers in here and scoop up the whole bunch. Meanwhile, until darkness came to cover his retreat, he would watch and learn, to give Cane as much information as possible.

He didn't learn much more over the next few hours, and the wait was tedious and uncomfortable. The heat was oppressive, and fire ants or some other kind of biting insects had found their way to his bare skin in spots. He had water, but not enough, and he was hungry. There was little visible activity in the camp, and his gaze wandered over the high ground opposite his position, on the other side of the camp. His eye caught a glint of light near the top of the opposite ridge. He focused on the spot and soon saw it again, light reflecting off of something. Something like binoculars.

Someone was hidden among the rocks, scanning with binoculars. He'd gone in an instant from watcher to, perhaps, watched, and his body tensed. Had he been seen? He'd be hard to spot where he was, even with binoculars, but if he could see the reflection from the binoculars, then the man behind those binoculars could see him if he looked in the right place.

But perhaps Binoculars wasn't a sentry from the camp at all. Bowman had been watching the camp all day, and knew that Binoculars hadn't climbed to his position from the camp, at least not since Bowman had been here, and there had been no activity in the camp to suggest an alert. It would be an odd position for a sentry. The high ground could be scanned just as easily from the camp, without the blind spots that Binoculars would have to his immediate left and right, as well as above and behind him. Bowman concluded that Binoculars was probably observing the camp, just as he was, and relaxed a bit. Bowman looked more carefully at the remainder of the high ground around the camp. He wasn't in a position to see it all, but didn't detect any other flashes of light, or any movement, in the areas that he could see. Had the cavalry already arrived? Was Binoculars their scout? He would wait and see. He couldn't move from his position in any case, while Binoculars' intentions were unclear and any movement could be spotted from the camp.

But Binoculars wasn't a sentry or a scout. Shortly after dark, he moved from his position. Bowman tensed again, thinking that Binoculars might be trying to circle around behind him, but it soon became clear that he was moving towards the camp, alone. At first, Bowman could just detect movement from time to time in the moonlight. As Binoculars got farther down the slope and closer to the camp, and to Bowman's position, Bowman could see that he was moving from cover to cover, slowly and carefully. The cover he chose blocked him from the view of anyone in the camp, but not from Bowman, with his higher vantage point. Bowman couldn't tell if he was armed, but he didn't carry a rifle. If he was some kind of lawman, he wasn't in uniform. He wore tan khaki pants, a dark, long-sleeved shirt and a dark brown or black cowboy hat. He had left his binoculars behind.

The camp's six main buildings were arranged along a dusty central avenue about forty feet wide. Bowman was looking almost straight down the avenue, towards the abandoned mine shaft in the opposite slope. The middle building on the right was the garage, and next to it, closer to Bowman, was the generator shed. The nearest two buildings on his left were the other two new buildings.

Binoculars had worked his way to his end of the row of buildings on Bowman's right, the side with the garage and the generator shed, when Bowman lost sight of him among the buildings. Bowman wondered what he was up to. Was he trying to get a closer look at the men in the camp?

About ten minutes later, the low hum of the generator stopped. The sound had been barely audible, and Bowman had ceased to be conscious of it during the long day, so when it went silent it took him a moment to understand what had changed. The men in the camp noticed immediately, however, and in a few seconds the door to one of the new buildings on the left opened and one of the Hispanic men emerged and walked towards the shed. He carried a rifle, but didn't look suspicious or alarmed. Bowman guessed that the generator cut out from time to time, as it ran out of fuel or for some other reason. Once at the shed, he opened the door and stepped inside, holding his rifle casually at his side.

Bowman figured that Binoculars had sabotaged the generator as a diversion, and that he would now be snooping around some other part of the camp. He was wrong.

Before the door to the generator shed had even swung shut behind the man, Bowman heard a scream. The scream was cut short, ending in a kind of gurgling groan, but it was enough to alert the entire camp. At least eight armed men ran out of the two occupied buildings, running towards the shed and shouting in English and Spanish. It was happening too quickly for Bowman to get an accurate count or keep track of the positions of all of the men. The fastest two, who were dressed like Gordon and the others, were shot down in the middle of the avenue, and the rest scattered for cover behind buildings or abandoned equipment and started to return fire. One of the two men in the middle of the avenue lay still. The other writhed and screamed in pain. The shots that had taken down the two had sounded like rifle shots. Bowman couldn't see Binoculars, who was between the nearest abandoned building and the garage, but figured that he'd cut the first man's throat, taken his rifle and used it on the others.

He also figured that he didn't have a dog in this fight. The men in the camp were up to no good, he was sure, but that didn't mean that Binoculars was on the side of the angels. Maybe he was a competitor, or someone with a personal grudge. Back in Iraq and Afghanistan they'd called this sort of thing, different factions of the enemy fighting each other, over ideology, territory, personality or whatever, red on red action. The thing to do was stay out of the way and hope for casualties on both sides.

Whatever plan Binoculars may have had was ruined by the first man's scream. He was outnumbered and was rapidly being outflanked and surrounded. Amid the sharp cracks of rifle fire and the shouting of men, Bowman could see men moving around the abandoned building nearest him, on Binoculars' left, and assumed others were outflanking him from his right as well, while still others kept him pinned down from across the avenue to his front. While this was happening, the man in the dirt stopped screaming and lay still.

Binoculars had made a solo attack on an armed camp, and it was about to end badly for him. How could he have imagined that it could end any other way? Who was he, and why had he done it? It didn't make any sense.

It was all over in a few minutes. The firing stopped, but the shouting continued. Two men dragged Binoculars, now without his hat, out into the avenue from between the buildings, while others scoured the area, looking for any friends Binoculars might have brought with him. Bowman didn't fit that description, but that wouldn't matter if they found him, and he froze in place and hoped they wouldn't widen their search beyond the camp itself. They didn't, and he slowly began to relax.

Binoculars was still alive, but he was clearly in pain and unable to stand. The two men carrying him threw him down in the dust and started to kick him in the ribs and the head. The door of the middle building on the left opened and one of the Hispanic men walked out, holding a pistol at his side. He was a short, dark, stocky man, and he looked like the boss, judging by his body language and that of the others.

The short man walked over to Binoculars, who was sprawled in the dirt. He reached down, grabbed

Binoculars by the hair and pulled his head back to look at his face. He shouted something in Spanish, and sounded very angry. Bowman couldn't understand much, but did hear a name, repeated at least twice, apparently referring to the man in the dirt. "Señor Walker."

So he must be Bill Walker, the DEA agent, whose wife and daughter had been murdered. But how had he found this place, and why had he come alone? Now Bowman did have a dog in this fight, but there was nothing he could do for now but watch in helpless frustration. Maybe there would be an opportunity to help later.

Down at the mining camp the short man – Bowman was now convinced that he was El Chato himself – said something to the two men who had been carrying Walker, and they pulled him up again and forced him to his knees. El Chato raised his pistol and pointed it at Walker's head. The gun bucked and roared, and Walker fell on his face in the dust.

CHAPTER 10

Kandahar Province, Republic of Afghanistan (2010)

"Don't leave me, Robbie!"

"I won't leave you, Boone. I'm right here."

"It hurts. It hurts bad."

"I know, but I can't give you any more morphine. We'll be out of here soon, and get you all fixed up."

Clayton Boone lapsed back into silence, apart from the constant low moan and the rasping of his breath. He sat with his back against the cinder block wall of the house, his legs flat on the floor. From time to time, his head would flop down on this chest, but then he would recover a little and hold it up again. If he didn't do so immediately, Bowman would shake him by the shoulder until he revived. Sometimes we die because we have no choice. Sometimes we die because it's easier.

Bowman had done what he could for him. The grenade had lacerated Boone's face from the bridge of his nose to the middle of his forehead, where the edge of his helmet had been. His body armor was a shredded mess, but had protected the parts of him that it covered. His legs were riddled with shrapnel, and at least one fragment had penetrated his chest cavity, from under his right armpit. The morphine had stopped the screaming, and Bowman had bandaged, as well as he could, the mess around Boone's eyes. The surgeons might be able to save one or both of them, but for now they were useless. The other wounds were not bleeding badly anymore, and would have to wait.

Robbie Bowman and Clayton Boone had clicked right away, and had been inseparable since they'd met a few years previously. Bowman didn't know why. They were very different in some ways. Bowman was quiet and reserved. Boone was gregarious, talked constantly, and would talk to anyone. Bowman liked to read, but had never seen Boone read anything, apart from an occasional magazine.

Bowman took another quick look out the window, saw nothing, and pulled his head back down. He was covering the approaches to this side of the house, relying on his squad mates in the other rooms to cover the other approaches. Bowman felt a strong urge to scream, to kick something, to give vent to his fear and anguish, but he had to hold it together and stay in the fight. The Talibs were out there, in ditches or behind rocks or sections of mud brick wall, about a hundred yards out. If the enemy fighters could work their way in to about fifty yards or closer, his odds of surviving another day would get a lot longer. At that distance, they could use grenades, and at that distance even the Talibs could shoot straight. Bowman's job was to make sure they didn't get that close. He wasn't afraid for himself. He didn't care anymore. They could have this fucking country and bury him in it. But Boone and the others were relying on him.

A Talib had broken from cover just after dawn and run for a stone wall closer to the house. Now he was lying in a heap about seventy yards out, looking like a pile of dirty rags. His sandaled feet protruded from the pile towards Bowman, and his bearded chin was just visible over the top. Bowman had to look at it every time he popped his head up to scan his sector.

It had been easier in the dark. His squad's night vision scopes had given them an advantage that the enemy respected, and after experiencing a few well-aimed shots, the Talibs kept to cover and limited themselves to occasional pot shots that seemed to hit the outside walls of the house at random, or even miss the house altogether. In daylight it was different. The Talibs were not good marksmen, but they could shoot well enough to make it dangerous to leave any body parts exposed for more than a moment. If they'd been trained in fire and movement, one squad providing covering fire while another advanced, they might have overrun the house by now.

Boone stirred, and raised his head weakly. "You still there, Robbie? You won't leave me, will you?"

Bowman turned from the window, sat back against the wall next to Boone and took hold of his hand. Both their hands were sticky with Boone's blood, and it felt like they were glued together.

"No, Boone, I won't leave you. We'll both get out of here real soon. The Lieutenant called for some backup, and a ride for you. They'll be right along." How soon, Bowman knew, depended upon what kind of resistance they were running into. It could be any minute, but it could also be hours. Bowman never doubted that their brothers would come and get them out of there, but he wasn't sure that he and Boone would survive until then.

Their squad had targeted the house he currently occupied the night before, at about three in the morning. That was supposed to be when the occupants would be least alert. They'd been told that this house was a safe house for Taliban operating in the area. The plan had been to kill or capture any Talibs they found and then get out before any organized resistance could develop. The squad had stacked up beside the door, kicked it down and rushed in, by the book. Bowman had been the first through the door. The two Talibs on the ground floor had scrambled up from the floor with their AK-47s, but it was dark and they were panicked. They just sprayed bullets in the general direction of the sound, and Bowman and the men right behind him killed them before they could do any damage. They were still down there, slumped in a corner.

Bowman disengaged his hand from Boone's, raised his head over the window sill again and quickly scanned with his scope. He spotted a head topped by a light brown pakol, or Afghan cap, peering from over a large rock, and he squeezed off a round. His round chipped the rock inches from the head, and it vanished back behind the rock. The frequency of the firing from the other rooms suggested that the rest of the squad was doing something similar. Occasionally, he would hear a curse from Ace or some muttered conversation from other parts of the house, but mostly they were silent.

Boone felt for the little gold Jesus around his neck and held it briefly before letting his hand fall back into his lap. "Robbie – you remember that time . . .?" Boone's voice trailed off, and his head slumped again.

"Stay with me, Boone," Bowman said as he shook him by the shoulder. He wondered what time Boone was thinking of. There were any number to choose from.

Maybe Boone was thinking of that time they abandoned the old '89 Lincoln Town Car on the ice near Fort Drum. Fort Drum was the home of the Tenth Mountain Division, in northern New York State, and their unit had been sent up there for six weeks of arctic warfare training. They'd bought that rusty old Lincoln from a local guy for two hundred dollars, one hundred each, but the cost and hassle of the frequent repairs was more than it was worth. One day, a few days before they were due to leave, they were in one of the local bars, more than a little drunk, and decided to drive the Lincoln out on the ice of a nearby lake and let it sink when the ice gave out. Giggling like a couple of little girls, they drove it out to the middle of the lake, going slowly and with the windows rolled down despite the cold. They'd seen ice fishing huts and snow machines out on the ice, so they thought it could hold the car, at least for a while. If the ice started to go, they'd be able to get out quickly through the open windows. The ice held, and they walked back to shore, slipping and falling on their asses from time to time, still laughing. The Lincoln fell through the ice sometime during the next afternoon, they heard.

Or maybe he was thinking of that time in Iraq when Bowman's canteen had taken an AK round. He and Boone had been engaged in a firefight with some locals who had ambushed their patrol. They were returning fire from behind cover, Bowman from behind the engine block of a Humvee, Boone a few feet away behind a low stone wall. Boone had run out of water, and Bowman was passing him his canteen when it was shot out of his hand and exploded, spraying water over both of them. Boone thought that was the funniest thing he'd ever seen. He told that story every chance he got, and the story got better each time, with more and better sound effects and telling details. Boone had always been a good story teller.

After they were out, Boone was going to come to Montana and go elk hunting with Robbie and his dad. Robbie was going to visit Boone in West Virginia for some coon hunting. But none of that could happen if he let Boone die here in this God forsaken shithole of a house in this God forsaken shithole of a country. Where was the fucking cavalry?

"How're you doing in there, Bowman?" It was the Lieutenant, from one of the other upstairs rooms.

"So far, so good, Sir, speaking for myself," Bowman said, trying to keep the anxiety out of his voice, and only partly succeeding. He didn't want to say out loud how he thought Boone was doing, but he knew the Lieutenant would read between the lines. "Any word on relief?"

"Two Strykers on the way. An MEV for Boone and an

ICV for us. Maybe ten minutes out."

The cavalry, at last. The Stryker was a good friend to have in a tight spot. It was an eight-wheeled armored personnel carrier that came in a variety of configurations. The MEV was a medical evacuation vehicle, basically an armored ambulance. The ICV was an infantry carrier vehicle, which carried a squad of nine and some heavy weaponry, usually a fifty-caliber Browning machine gun. Boone would be evacuated in the MEV, and the ICV would help the rest of them kill or scatter the enemy. It wasn't quite a tank, but it could bring some serious hurt. They were going to be make it.

Boone stirred a little now, and coughed. Pink foam bubbled between his slightly parted lips. Damn it, thought Bowman, God damn it.

Clearing the top floor had been harder than the ground floor. There had been three Talibs up there, and they were now fully alert. The Talibs upstairs didn't have night vision gear, but they saw well enough in the dark at such close range. They covered the only stairway with their AKs, and tossed an occasional grenade. It took about twenty minutes for the squad to kill two of them, and the third one retreated to one of the three upstairs rooms. Bowman and Boone had been assigned to clear this room.

No one knew if there were any civilians in the house, so just tossing a grenade into the room wasn't an option. Not this time. They would have to go in and root him out.

Since Bowman had gone in first through the front door, Boone went in first now. No one volunteered or was ordered to go in first. There was a protocol, and it was Boone's turn. Bowman was right behind Boone, but the grenade went off the instant Boone burst through the door. The guy must have been holding it with the pin out and the timer cooked off, and just released the handle when the door burst open.

They'd shoved what was left of him off into a corner, as far from Bowman and Boone as possible. Bowman couldn't even hate him for what he'd done, although he'd tried. It just all seemed so pointless.

Bowman knew that if he hadn't killed the woman and child in Iraq, they would've tossed a grenade into this room, and Boone would not be slumped against the wall with a ruined face. That was the truth, and there was no getting around it.

Almost as soon as the house had been cleared, they started taking fire from the surrounding fields, and here they were.

Boone seemed to perk up a little, and said "Ma, is that you?"

"It's Robbie, Boone."

"Help me, Ma. I can't see."

"Hang in there, Boone, please," Bowman pleaded. "Just a few more minutes."

"It hurts, Ma. It hurts something awful."

"I know, I know, I'm sorry."

Boone shuddered suddenly, and a torrent of bright red blood poured out of his mouth and spilled down his chin and over his chest. "No! No! No! Noooo!" Bowman cried. He tossed aside his rifle and tried to stop the blood by clamping his hand over Boone's mouth, but the hot blood just backed up and came pouring out of his nose and over Bowman's hand. Realizing the futility of what he was doing, he took his hand from Boone's mouth and pulled him to his chest in a tight embrace as Boone went slack and his rasping breath stopped.

Bowman was vaguely aware of Murphy entering the room and taking up the position at the window that Bowman had abandoned. Murphy didn't say anything, and kept his gaze averted from Bowman and Boone.

With Boone in his arms, and soaked in his warm blood, Bowman threw his head back and uttered a long, guttural groan as tears ran down his face, mingled with the mucous running from his nose and carved channels in the crusted dirt and blood on his face and neck. Then he dropped his

85

head and buried his face in the top of Boone's head.

"Don't leave me, Boone," Bowman sobbed. "Don't leave me."

CHAPTER 11

Now he was in another desert, on the other side of the world, but he hadn't escaped the violence and death. The shooting of Walker shocked Bowman. He'd seen men killed in combat, but never executed like that, in cold blood. He'd seen the aftermath of executions, both in Iraq and Afghanistan. The bad guys would sweep through an area, and anyone suspected of collaborating with the Americans would be forced to kneel and then shot in the back of the head in front of their families and neighbors. The Americans would come back through the next day, too late to be of any help. He'd even recognized some of the victims, locals who had smiled at him, or offered him sweet tea. Maybe that was all it took to get them killed. It had bothered him, of course. It had bothered him a lot. But seeing it happen was different.

And there was another difference, one that, he was almost too ashamed to acknowledge, even to himself, made it more horrific. The other victims had been foreigners, and it had happened in a foreign land. This was America, his own land, and the victim this time was an American. Bowman had seen more than his share of death and suffering, but he thought he'd left that behind him when he'd left the service and come home. The last few days had brought back some unwelcome memories.

Immediately after Walker's body slumped forward into the dust, El Chato began shouting orders, and the men in the camp began moving purposefully in various directions. It soon became clear that they were packing up to go. They brought three black SUVs out of the garage and started to fill them with equipment and supplies from the other buildings. Someone got the generator running again, so that they'd have light while they packed up, Bowman presumed. One of the SUVs had a roof rack, and the bodies of the three men killed by Walker were wrapped in tarps and lashed to the roof rack. Walker's body was left where it lay. In less than half an hour, the three SUVs headed out of the camp and through the ring of hills to Bowman's left, trailing a cloud of dust. In their haste, they left the generator running, the lights on and the doors open.

There was nothing he could do for Walker now. All he could do was to get back to Tierra Roja as soon as he could, tell the authorities what he'd seen and let them take it from there. He'd do his duty as a good citizen and then get as far away from this place as he could. But he needed water and food, and he was pretty sure that El Chato had left some behind in his haste.

So, a few minutes after the last SUV had disappeared beyond the ring of hills, Bowman crawled out of his hiding place and worked his way down the slope to the camp. First he would check Walker, then gather up some supplies for the return journey. He had little doubt that Walker was dead, but he wanted to be able to tell Sheriff Cane that he'd checked.

Walker was lying on his stomach where he'd fallen, with his face to the side, away from Bowman as he approached. Bowman had expected him to be lying in a pool of his own blood, but he wasn't. He'd expected to see a gaping exit wound in the back of his head, but it looked intact. Bowman quickly ran the final few yards, knelt down by Walker and felt for a pulse at his carotid artery, on the side of his neck just under the jaw.

He found one. Walker was alive.

Before moving him, Bowman quickly scanned Walker for injuries. He saw what looked like entry wounds below his right shoulder and in his upper left thigh. He'd been shot from behind by one or more of the men who had outflanked him. The side of his face that Bowman could see, including most of his forehead, looked uninjured. Bowman didn't understand how that could be. He'd seen El Chato shoot him in the head. After finishing his examination, Bowman carefully turned Walker onto his back, and understood what had happened.

Either El Chato was a poor shot, or Walker had moved his head at the last second. The left side of Walker's head was plastered with blood and dirt, but looked intact. The bullet must have hit the side of Walker's head at a shallow angle and carved a gash along the skull, apparently without penetrating it. Apart from the gash, which was a superficial wound, the effect would've been like getting hit in the side of the head by a major league fastball. It was enough to knock him unconscious, which it had, and likely to cause a concussion. Swelling of the brain was possible, which could yet kill him if his other wounds didn't.

Bowman found the exit wounds corresponding to the entry wounds on Walker's chest and leg, and they looked clean. He couldn't tell how much damage was done internally, but this was promising. Those wounds looked like they came from the 5.56 millimeter full metal jacket rounds fired by the M4, which is why they hadn't mushroomed inside Walker, as an unjacketed round would, and left large exit wounds. The military full metal jacket round is designed to leave as small an injury channel as possible. The goal is to injure the enemy, not kill him. An injured man is more trouble to the enemy than a dead man, because he had to be cared for. Walker's head wound was likely caused by a nine-millimeter round, which would make a bigger hole, but it hadn't penetrated. It looked like the blood loss hadn't been extensive, apart from any possible internal bleeding.

He needed to do what he could for Walker with whatever he had with him or could find at the camp. After that, he could consider what to do next. He quickly reconnoitered the three habitable buildings and discovered that one of them had a number of cots and some piles of abandoned supplies. That would do. Bowman carried Walker into the building and laid him on one of the cots, then gathered up some towels and bottles of water that were among the abandoned supplies.

He cut away Walker's clothes to get at the wounds on his chest and leg, and cleaned and bandaged them with the towels. Then he did the same with the head wound. As he'd thought, the bullet hadn't penetrated the skull, but the skull was exposed for part of the length of the gash.

After he'd finished cleaning and bandaging the wounds, Bowman positioned Walker on his right side in the fetal position, with a rolled-up towel under his head for a pillow. Concussions could cause vomiting, and he didn't want Walker to choke on his own vomit, as he might do if he were lying on his back. He didn't think that the wound below Walker's right shoulder had involved the lungs, but he'd placed him on his right side, just in case. If his right lung was compromised, his left lung would have to do the job of both, and could to that better without the weight of his body pressing down on it. It probably hurt more to lie on his injured side, but Walker wasn't complaining.

Bowman didn't think there was anything more he could do for Walker for now. He found some energy bars and bottled water that had been left behind, and refueled and rehydrated while he considered his options. Could they stay here and wait for help? He had no way of calling for help, and no one knew they were here, unless Walker had left word with someone. That was possible, but he couldn't count on it. He needed to get Walker to a hospital quickly. Could he carry him back to Tierra Roja? Yes, he thought he could, but would Walker survive the journey? It had taken Bowman most of the night to walk here, and it would take him at least as long to get back if he were carrying Walker, no matter how hard he pushed himself. There might be a shorter route out to a town or road, perhaps following the tracks of El Chato's SUVs. The last thing he wanted, however, was to stumble upon them, so following their tracks would not do. And to head in some other direction, to strike out blindly into country he didn't know, was too risky. He'd have to stick with the route he knew, and go out the way he'd come in.

Much of the night was already gone, and it would be well into the heat of the day before he could make it back, if he were carrying Walker. More importantly, Bowman didn't think that Walker would survive being jolted and jarred on Bowman's back for several hours. No, there was only one real option. He'd have to leave Walker here and go back by himself for help. The code he'd lived by for eight years demanded that you never leave anyone behind, dead or alive, but he would have to do just that. If he pushed himself hard, he thought he could make it back in a little more than half the time it had taken him to get here. Given how much of the night had already passed, perhaps he could make it by dawn. Certainly he could get back on his own much faster than he could with Walker on his back, and a helicopter could be back here with medical help for Walker shortly after that. And if someone did know that Walker was here and came for him, he would be here when they arrived. Going back by himself was the only way.

Once he'd decided to go, he knew he must go quickly. He didn't know how long Walker could survive without medical attention. Maybe he would be too late, no matter how fast he was, and maybe he had plenty of time and didn't need to hurry. But he had to assume that Walker would live if he gave it his full effort, and would die if he did not. If his best efforts were not needed, or were not enough, he could live with that. What he could not live with was knowing, or suspecting, that he could have saved him if he'd only tried harder.

He thought of leaving his pack behind. He could move faster without the extra weight, but he decided that he needed it to carry water. He'd need a lot of water, and couldn't afford to spend time looking for it. Water would be the heaviest part of his load at first, but the load would lighten as he drank it. He kept his knife and a few other items that might be useful if he got in trouble in the desert, but took out his extra clothes and his book. It didn't seem like much of a weight savings, but it might make a difference. He put several bottles of water in his pack, along with a handful of the energy bars, and left some water and energy bars on a cot next to Walker, where he could easily see them and reach them if he regained consciousness.

He knew he couldn't run hard the entire way, so he settled into an easy lope that he hoped he could sustain for the six or seven hours that he thought would be required to reach Tierra Roja. It was probably twice his walking pace. At times he had to walk, where the ground was too broken, or the slope too extreme. He couldn't afford to break an ankle. But even his walking pace was forced, not like the leisurely stroll of the previous night.

Bowman retraced the route he'd taken on the previous night, more or less. When he started, the moon was nearly at its zenith in the south, so he kept it to his right. He was going east this time, rather than trying to remember the way he'd come, but he did recognize some landmarks, including the natural spring and cistern. He had water enough, if he rationed it carefully, and he didn't want to take the time to stop for more. He heard a lone coyote howl in the distance, but he didn't see any. It was a mournful sound, and it matched his mood.

This desert trek had seemed like an adventure the night before, but now it was torture. He'd been awake for about forty hours straight, and he was bone tired. His muscles ached, both from the exertion and from the enforced inactivity of the previous day, while he was holed up watching the mining camp. He was rationing his water, and he was thirsty. A blister was developing on the instep of his left foot. He was sunburned in spots, and various stinging or biting insects had found unprotected flesh to add to his discomfort. The desert in the moonlight didn't seem so magical anymore.

Still, he was young and strong, and the first couple of hours were bearable. After that, it got harder. His skin was raw where the straps of his backpack rubbed across his shoulders, and in several other places where his clothing rubbed repeatedly against his skin. The constant pounding was taking a toll on his joints, and his knees and hips ached. His calves were on fire. The backs of his thighs were tightening, and the fronts were aching. Even the inside of his elbows were sore, from the effort of keeping his arms up as he ran. The blisters on his feet were developing blisters of their own, and he felt like he was running on bloody stumps at the ends of his legs. He tried to shut out the pain, but found that he was walking more, and running less. Any roughness of the ground or slight rise became an excuse to walk for a while. And the pain was affecting his stride, which was slowing him down even when he was running.

Suddenly, his toe caught on a protruding rock, and he was falling. The natural reaction is to try to break your fall with your hands, to protect your face, but this could lead to injured wrists or broken collar bones, as he had learned to his cost. So as soon as he realized that he was falling, he tucked his arms into his body and twisted his torso to take the impact on his upper arm and shoulder. As he hit the ground, he continued the roll onto his back, until his momentum was stopped by his backpack.

Shaken by the fall, he lay on his back for a minute or two, to calm down and do an internal survey for injuries. He was lucky. The ground he had landed on was smooth and sandy, and he had sustained no injuries beyond minor abrasions. A rock in the wrong place would have made all the difference.

Slowly, he got to his feet and dusted himself off. His stumble, he knew, had been caused by his poor running form. He was not lifting his feet as much as he should, and that was due to the fatigue and pain. He had to do better than this.

He took off his pack and rummaged around inside until he found a small bottle of ibuprofen tablets. Bowman didn't like to take pain pills, especially for muscle or joint pain. Pain was a warning, and he tried to heed it. Otherwise, the trouble would compound. But he couldn't heed the warning now, despite the risk of further injury. He must push on through the pain, but he would try to deaden it a little. He shook out two tablets, considered for a moment, and then shook out four more. This was a special occasion. He swallowed the tablets, drank some water and ate an energy bar. Then he started off again.

The moon was about half way through its descent to the western horizon, which meant that it must be about three in the morning. He would need to push hard if he hoped to make it by dawn. In about fifteen minutes, he felt the ibuprofen begin to take effect. He felt much better, and picked up his pace. He'd take more tablets as needed, because he couldn't let himself slow down.

The ibuprofen had helped, and was still helping, he was sure, but soon enough the pain and fatigue had caught up and surpassed the previous level. Still he pressed on. What was the line? 'If you can fill each unforgiving minute with sixty seconds' worth of distance run,' or something like that. Tennyson? No, Kipling. He couldn't keep them straight. But that was the trick. Focus on this minute, get through it, then repeat. And each minute was more unforgiving than the last.

But why put himself through this? Did he even care whether Walker lived or died? Of course he did, but only in the abstract way one cares about the fate of strangers. He wasn't a brother-in-arms. He didn't know Walker, had never even spoken to him, and wouldn't miss him if he died. And he had just seen him kill three people. But this isn't about Walker, he told himself, it's about me. He had to know that he'd done all that could be done. He couldn't bear another such burden.

A little before dawn, he struck the road and started down it towards Tierra Roja. He refused to walk, because the road was flat and smooth, but his running form had degenerated into something more like a shuffle. There was no traffic, and he staggered on for about an hour without seeing anyone. The first vehicle he saw, driving out of the rising sun, was a Bronco County Sheriff's Department SUV. It was a welcome sight. What had come to feel like a death march was finally over. He flagged the car down and soon saw that it was driven by Deputy Abbott, who pulled to a stop next to Bowman and lowered his window.

"Back already, sir? You look like you've been through the ringer," he said, smiling.

Bowman skipped the usual formalities and blurted out his message in one breath, "Last night I saw Bill Walker, the DEA agent, get shot — out at an old mining camp in the middle of the desert. He was still alive when I left him. I patched him up as well as I could — and I've been running all night to get here. We need to get a medical helicopter out to him right away."

Instantly, Abbott's smile vanished and he was all business. "Get in the car, sir, and we'll go talk to the Sheriff."

Bowman climbed into the front passenger seat and Abbott made a U turn and headed back to town at speed. As soon as he was headed in the right direction, he got on the radio and told the dispatcher to alert the Sheriff.

"I've got Bowman with me. He says he saw Bill Walker get shot, up at the old silver mine. We need to get a medical helicopter in the air as soon as possible. We'll be there in five minutes."

It had never felt so good to sit down, to get off his feet. As long as he was off his feet and didn't move, there was almost no pain. To lie down would be even better. To sleep would be heaven itself. Had he done all that could be done? Had he filled each unforgiving minute? Yes, he thought he had.

Cane was waiting for them out front when they arrived. It was painful to stand up and walk, but Bowman managed to lurch up the stairs and into the station house, like a zombie, he thought. Cane and Abbott tried to help him, but he waved them off. He collapsed into a chair in Cane's office and quickly told him what he'd seen. Cane made a few quick calls, to the Bronco County Hospital, the DEA and the State Police.

"That should get things started," Cane said. "They'll get out there as quick as they can, to pick up Bill Walker and see if they can catch up with El Chato. That job's too big for the Sheriff's Department. With any luck, they'll get the whole lot of 'em."

Bowman nodded. He was emotionally and physically drained, and now that he'd passed the baton, he could surrender to his fatigue. "Sheriff, if you're done with me, I think I'll go get something to eat and check back into the motel. I need a nap."

"I can tell, son. You've had a busy couple of days. Tell you what, DEA and the State Police will want a full statement from you once they've checked out the mining camp, so that'll be towards the end of the day, I expect. We've got a shower here, and you can use a bed in the cell to take a nap. While you're taking a shower, we'll get some breakfast for you, and then you can sleep as long as you like. You're free to go, of course, but this way you save some money and we know where to find you when we're ready for your statement."

"Thank you, Sheriff, that sounds great."

Abbott helped Bowman out of his chair and led him out of Cane's office and towards the shower room, with Bowman leaning on his shoulder for support. Mrs. Flores saw them pass and followed. Once they reached the shower room, she told Abbott that she would take it from there.

She was friendly now, unlike the last time he'd seen her, and she made sure he had towels, toiletries, a pillow and everything else he needed, including alcohol pads and a pin, so that he could drain the blisters on his feet that hadn't already burst. She gave him one of the orange jumpsuits to wear as pajamas and told him to leave his dirty clothes by the shower. When he pulled off his boots to reveal socks soaked in blood, she gasped, "Ay dios mio," and made the sign of the cross. When he peeled off his socks to reveal his bloody, swollen and blistered feet and purple toenails, she nearly fainted. She noticed his sun burn and insect bites, and brought him some lotion to take away the sting. He felt like a chick under the wing of a mother hen, something he hadn't felt in a long time.

He was exhausted, and as soon as he'd showered, done what he could for his blistered feet, and eaten two breakfast burritos, he fell into a deep sleep. And it was like falling, not like drifting. It was like hurtling down into a dark, bottomless void, a welcome and welcoming void.

CHAPTER 12

DEA Special Agent Clementine Bates spoke into the mouthpiece attached to her headset. It was the only way to make herself heard over the roar of the Blackhawk's engine and rotors.

"We're all strapped in back here. Let's go."

The call from Sheriff Cane had come in about an hour ago, and she'd spent that hour securing this helicopter and putting this team together. The DEA didn't have a dedicated SWAT team, but every agent was trained in the same weapons and tactics. This was an ad hoc team put together on the spot. The New Mexico State Police did have a dedicated SWAT team – they called it the Tactical Team – but they didn't have a suitable helicopter available. DEA in El Paso did not normally have access to a Blackhawk helicopter, but this one was passing through on its way to South America and Bates had been able to secure it for this mission. So Bates and Detective Carrillo had agreed that this would be a DEA operation. In addition to the two pilots and her, there were eight special agents on board. She and the other special agents wore body armor and headsets that tied into the helicopter's intercom system. Each carried an assault rifle and a pistol.

If what Cane had said was correct, this firepower would be needed if they caught up with El Chato.

As the Blackhawk's rotor blades began to bite and it rose slowly into the air, the radio crackled, "DEA El Paso, this is Air Ambulance One out of Bronco County Hospital. We are five minutes out from rendezvous. Please advise your location and ETA. Over."

That was to be expected, thought Bates. The air ambulance would be standing by at all times, and was closer. She flipped her microphone from internal to external and said, "This is DEA El Paso. We are just leaving El Paso, and will be at the rendezvous in less than one hour. Do not approach until we have arrived to secure the scene. Over." Those were standing orders. The safety and security of the rescue team must come first. Otherwise, an attempted rescue of one man could lead to the deaths of several others.

"DEA El Paso, we were told that the bad guys had left. One hour may be too late for the patient. Please clarify. Over."

"Air Ambulance One, we don't know for certain that there's no opposition on the ground. We cannot allow you to land until we're certain. Over."

There was only silence from Air Ambulance One for several minutes, then the radio crackled again, "DEA El Paso, we have arrived at the rendezvous and see no activity. Flight Paramedic, Flight Nurse and I are agreed to land. Over."

"Air Ambulance One, I say again, do not land until we arrive to support. Over."

"And I say again, we're landing. Over and out."

Good for you, Bates thought. I hope I would do the same in your shoes. She also hoped that there would be no nasty surprises awaiting them.

Bates went over in her mind what Cane had told her. This guy Robert Bowman had witnessed the shooting of Walker, found that he was still alive, and then run all the way back to Tierra Roja, arriving just at dawn. That must be more than twenty miles, as the crow flies. But he couldn't run in a straight line, as the crow is supposed to fly. He'd have had to maneuver around terrain, and adjust his direction from time to time. She guessed that the total distance he'd run must be close to the marathon distance of twenty-six point two miles. And he'd run it in five or six hours.

Bates was an experienced runner, so she knew what it takes. A six-hour time for a trail marathon would put you in the middle of the pack of very dedicated athletes. Bowman had had no trail to follow. He cut straight across country, through rough terrain, carrying a heavy pack and wearing boots.

Long-distance running, except at the elite levels, wasn't so much about speed as about the ability to keep going when all you wanted to do was stop. To ignore the voice in your head that keeps whispering, 'Why am I doing this?' The last couple of hours for Bowman must have been painful. And all the time, he couldn't know if his efforts would do any good. Walker might already be dead, or might live to be an old man without any help from Bowman. No one would've blamed him if he'd walked the whole way back. It was a tremendous effort of will, and a demonstration of character. She was looking forward to meeting this man.

They were about ten minutes out from the mining camp when the radio crackled again.

"DEA El Paso, this is Air Ambulance One. We have located patient. He is alive but unresponsive. He has been stabilized and secured aboard. Preparing to lift off. Over."

Bates felt a wave of relief flow through her. She'd tried to put her personal feelings aside and concentrate on the job at hand, but now that the tension was relieved she realized just how tense she'd been. She knew Walker, and had worked with him many times. He was several years her senior, and had acted as an unofficial mentor. She'd seen him once since the murder of his wife and child. There was nothing useful she could say to him, of course. She'd muttered some banal condolences, but she wasn't sure he even recognized her. He'd looked haunted, and his eyes had a vacant look, like there was nobody home. El Paso had put him on temporary medical leave and had made him turn in his gun, for his own protection.

If what Bowman had said was correct, it looked like Walker was now a murderer himself. Some murders are worse than others, but it was still murder, and she wasn't sure how to feel about that. She doubted that he would be prosecuted, if he lived, and he could probably argue temporary insanity if he were. She knew that what he'd done was wrong, but couldn't judge him harshly under the circumstances. Temporary insanity. Yes, she would go with that.

"Air Ambulance One, this is DEA El Paso," she said. "Any sign of activity at the site? Over."

"Negative. The site is all yours. En Route to Bronco County Hospital. Over."

"Good work. And thank you. Over and out."

By the time they arrived at the mining camp, the medivac helicopter was out of sight. They could see from the effects of the rotor wash that it had landed in the middle of the central avenue. It looked like someone had raked a large circle clean. They landed in the same spot and quickly jumped out and formed a perimeter. She didn't doubt that El Chato and his people were long gone, but she would play it by the book until she'd checked for herself. Bates, Johnson and Spitz stayed with the helicopter, on the perimeter. One squad of three checked the buildings on one side of the avenue, and the other squad checked those on the other side. Within five minutes, the two squads returned to the helicopter and reported all clear.

Clementine Bates walked up close to the pilot's

window, so she could be heard now that she was no longer connected to the intercom, and said, "I want you to see if you can find the tracks of their vehicles and follow them. I'll send everyone except myself, Johnson and Spitz with you. If you spot them, use your discretion as to whether to engage or just observe and report. My guess is that they're long gone, and the best you can do is follow the track out to the road. That itself will be helpful."

"Roger that. When I come back, I'll circle a bit to reconnoiter the area."

Bates didn't mind the suggestion. She was in charge of this operation because she'd been assigned to the investigation of the Walker killings, but she didn't outrank anyone here. Most of these men – she was the only woman along – had more experience than her. The helicopter pilot certainly knew more than she did about the best use for a helicopter. That was one of the things she liked about this job. She'd joined the Drug Enforcement Administration right out of college. It sounded exciting, and she didn't know what else to do with a degree in psychology. It was exciting, often enough, and very rewarding. She'd only been on the job for six years, and was in charge of this operation. From what she'd heard, that wouldn't happen at most other government agencies.

"Good idea. As soon as the other six are back on board, you can lift off. When you come back, the rest of us will get back on board and we'll take a look around."

She asked Johnson and Spitz to remain with her, and sent the others to the helicopter, which soon lifted off. Her plan was to go through the camp to look for actionable intelligence, such as evidence of where El Chato might have gone, and any obvious evidence of criminal activity, like drugs. A full crime scene investigation unit would be out here as soon as it could be arranged, and they'd do the detail work, like dusting for fingerprints and collecting samples of the blood that had been shed. Her goal was to get a sense for what was going on here, and what had happened the night before.

The first building they checked was the one where Walker had lain, which consisted of just one large room. There were several cots, but it was clear which one he had occupied. Space had been cleared around it, and the floor around it was littered with bloody towels and the wrappings from medical supplies used by the medivac crew, like needles and bandages. There was a spray of vomit to one side of the cot, which looked to be at least a couple of hours old.

"He's lucky he didn't choke on that," Spitz said.

"Sure was," Bates said, but she thought it was probably more than just luck.

On one of the other cots she saw a small pile of clothing, with a book on top. Bowman lightening his load. He must have known what he was in for.

A small table and four chairs sat in a corner of the room. It looked like they'd been playing cards and hadn't taken the time to gather them up when they left, though they'd taken the time to collect the pot, if there had been any. Two of the hands were face down and neatly stacked. Looks like those two had folded, she thought. The other two hands were face up and fanned out to show all of the cards. Both showed two pair. One of them showed a pair of kings and a pair of jacks.

The other hand was the winner: aces and eights.

Nothing else in the building was of interest to her, but she knew that the CSI team would find plenty of evidence that could be used to identify the occupants, if they were located.

The next building had only three cots, so it must have been the one occupied by El Chato and the other Mexicans. One small room looked like a pantry and was equipped with a fitting for a padlock, but it was missing and the door was standing open. The shelves inside were bare, but she was certain that the CSI team would find residue of heroin.

"Smell that?" she said. She could still detect the distinctive vinegar odor.

"Yes, indeed," said Johnson. "There must have been a tidy pile of smack in here not long ago." Spitz nodded in agreement.

El Chato had left some miscellaneous trash behind, but they found no papers or anything else that might lead them to his new hideout. The garage held nothing but supplies, and the buildings that hadn't been renovated held nothing at all.

It looked like most of the fighting had occurred around the generator shed. The generator wasn't running, and had likely run out of gas. Just inside the door was a large pool of blood, now dry or congealing. In the pool of blood lay a hunting knife. Outside, there were a few blood spots, several shell casings and Walker's hat. It all fit with what Bowman had told Cane, and Cane had told her.

One more thing to check, thought Bates. Leaving Spitz and Johnson at the camp, she climbed the hill above the mine shaft, looked around for a few minutes, and then returned with Walker's binoculars. Then she retrieved his hat. He'll want his hat back.

By then, the helicopter had returned and they all climbed aboard. The pilot flew in an outward spiral as they scanned the area. He pointed out the track taken by the SUVs.

"That track comes out on an isolated stretch of Old County Road. No way to follow after that. They could be hundreds of miles away by now. I logged the GPS coordinates of the intersection with the road."

"Roger that," Bates said into her mouthpiece, "We'll get the CSI team to come up by that route."

Apart from the track of the SUVs, there was little to see for several miles out from the mining camp except the desert terrain, until they spotted the truck. It was a black pickup truck, about five miles west of the camp, parked next to a long escarpment running north to south. Bates recognized it as Walker's, and guessed that he'd driven it out here across country and stopped here because the terrain had become too rough for his truck. He must have walked the last five miles or so.

"Can you put us down near that truck?"

"Roger that."

"No need to power down; I'll just be a minute," she said, as the pilot put the chopper down in a dirty cloud. She jumped down and ran crouched towards the truck, squinting and holding her breath against the grit and dust. Once she was clear of the rotor wash, she straightened up and blinked the dust out of her eyes.

It was Walker's truck, all right, a Ford F-150. The keys were still in it, and his phone was on the seat.

Bates turned it on. The background was a picture of a young woman and a little girl, smiling into the camera. Bates recognized Mary and Emma from pictures that Walker kept at work. What a pretty little girl, she thought. Who could do such a thing? He'd had that picture fresh in his mind as he walked towards the mining camp.

The phone required a code to access, which she didn't know, but she could see that it was low on power and that there was no reception. He must have figured that there was no point in taking it with him. Reception wasn't going to get any better deeper into the desert.

There was nothing else of interest, so she pocketed the phone and headed back to the chopper. Maybe there would be some messages or phone logs that would help explain why Walker had decided to come out here. She'd send someone back for the truck.

Spitz gave her a hand up into the chopper, and she strapped herself back in. As they lifted off, she thought about what was next. Once they were back in El Paso, she would need to drive up to Tierra Roja to compare notes with Sheriff Cane and Detective Carrillo, and to interview Robert Bowman.

CHAPTER 13

It was the middle of the afternoon when Bowman awoke. He'd slept for only a few hours, but it was the best sleep he'd had in a long time, and he felt refreshed. There had been no dreams, and that made all the difference. They seemed to drain all the rest out of sleep. Was it because he had been so exhausted? He hoped it was not just that.

His clothes had been washed, and were folded neatly and lying on the other bottom bunk. He shed the orange jumpsuit and dressed carefully. His fatigued muscles had stiffened while he slept, and it was painful to move, at first. The blisters on his feet had filled with fluid again, and he lanced and drained them again before putting on his socks and boots. His feet were still a little sore, but that would pass. He'd probably lose a few toenails, but they'd grow back.

The station was empty, except for the dispatcher in his cubicle and Cane in his office. The door to his office was open, and he was on the phone. When he saw Bowman hovering outside, he said into the phone, "Hold on a sec," then put his hand over the receiver and looked up at Bowman inquiringly.

"I'm just going to walk over to the diner and get some lunch, Sheriff. Be back soon."

Cane just nodded and returned his attention to his phone conversation, so Bowman walked out the front door. Just that morning he'd felt that he wouldn't be able to walk again for a week, at least. But now, after his shower and nap, he felt almost fully recovered. The diner, he recalled, was just a short walk away, on Main Street, and he set off in that direction.

Hank's Diner was a version of the American classic, shaped like a railroad car and generously decorated with chrome on the outside. The doors were up a few steps in the center of the building, and a row of windows stretched the length of the building on either side. Bowman guessed that it dated from the fifties or sixties.

Inside, a row of booths lined the front wall, under the windows. Across from the booths a counter stretched the length of the building, with stools bolted to the floor. He smelled coffee, frying bacon and a pot of chili simmering on the stove, and his mouth watered. He was hungry. As Bowman entered, the short order cook looked up from the griddle and gave him a quick nod. Bowman had been there a couple of times already, and the cook recognized him. He was a short, fat man dressed all in white, including an apron over a tee shirt and a paper hat. He was a classic, just like the diner itself. Bowman loved these kinds of places. They were simple and unpretentious, but at the same time had style. The food was never fancy, but what they did, they usually did well.

It was past the usual lunch hour, and there were only a few other customers in the place, a couple of men at the counter who could be construction workers or truck drivers, an older couple in one of the booths to the left of the door and, in a booth to the right of the door, Mrs. Flores. She sat on the side of the booth facing the door, and smiled at him as he entered. It looked like she'd just finished eating, and was finishing up her coffee. He walked over and said, "Mind if I join you, Mrs. Flores?"

"Please do, Robbie," she said, gesturing at the bench opposite her.

That morning Bowman had insisted that she stop calling him 'Mr. Bowman.' It didn't feel right for a woman who could've been his mother to call him that. In fact, it felt a little strange to him to hear anyone call him that. He'd joined the military as a teenager, and in the military he was 'Robbie' to his friends and 'Bowman' or 'Corporal' to everyone else.

"Do you feel better after your nap?" she said, as he slid into the booth opposite her.

"Much better. I slept like a rock. Thank you for washing my clothes."

The waitress now appeared. She was a middle-aged woman in a faded blue dress and a blue and white checked apron, the same woman who had taken his order the other times he'd been there. "What can I get for you, Hon'? It's on the house," she said, one hand holding her order pad and the other ready with a pencil. She was smiling. He didn't think he'd seen her smile before.

"On the house?"

"That's right. We heard what you did for Bill Walker. Boss says your money's no good here." She nodded in the direction of the short order cook.

Bowman looked over and the cook gave him a little salute. Word gets around fast.

"Thanks. That's very nice of you," he said to the waitress. "I'll have a grilled cheese sandwich and a bowl of that chili that smells so good, and some coffee." She nodded and walked off.

After she was gone, Mrs. Flores said, "Did the Sheriff tell you about Mr. Walker?"

"No, he was on the phone when I left. What have you heard?"

"He is alive, and at the County Hospital now. They say he is expected to live, but he would not have lasted much longer. You saved his life, Robbie. You are a hero to this town." She smiled at him, and then continued, a little sheepishly, "I cannot believe I thought you were the killer. I am sorry about that."

"You and everyone else, ma'am. There's nothing to be sorry about."

"But I should have been able to tell by looking at you that you would not be capable of something like that. But at first I did not look at you properly."

"I hope you're right, but I think we're all capable of doing terrible things, if pushed hard enough. I'm no murderer, but I've done things that I'm not proud of." Bowman was surprised at himself for opening up like this, but Mrs. Flores seemed so sympathetic that it drew him out. Maybe I've been looking for a chance to talk to someone, he thought.

Mrs. Flores looked at him closely, deep concern evident in her face. "I do not doubt that you have seen some horrible things, Robbie, and maybe you have been forced to do some things that trouble you, but I know that you are a good person. I can see it in your eyes."

"My eyes?"

"Yes. You have kind eyes. Kind, but a little sad. I will pray for you, Robbie. I will ask God to take away the sadness."

Bowman felt naked and exposed, and embarrassed. He said nothing for a long while, but just looked down at the table top and tried to pull himself together. He hoped he was kind – he tried to be – and yes, he was a little sad. That's probably not the way he would've put it, but it was accurate enough.

After a while, Mrs. Flores said, "You remind me of my son, Fernando. He died a couple of years ago. He was about your age, and about your size too. He was a good boy, and he also had kind eyes."

"I'm sorry, ma'am," Bowman said, finally looking up from the table.

"Thank you," she said, and smiled sadly. "He died of the heroin. Before the heroin he had never used any drugs, or been in any trouble with the law. He was a good boy. And then he had a motorcycle accident and was badly hurt. They are too dangerous, I told him, but of course he did not listen. In the hospital he became addicted to the pain killers, and after he was out of the hospital he started with the heroin. We did not even know it until he died."

"I'm sorry," Bowman said again. Fernando must be the son of a friend that Sheriff Cane had mentioned.

"He is with God now, and I will see him soon enough. Until then, it is a cross I must bear." She fingered the small silver cross she wore around her neck. "He was training to be a carpenter, like his father. They worked together, my husband and him. We miss him very much."

I'm not the only one who is a little sad, thought Bowman. Bowman felt like he needed to say something, but didn't know what to say. "Do you have any other children, ma'am?" As soon as he said it, Bowman realized that it was exactly the wrong thing to say. He'd have given a great deal for the chance to take it back, but there are no do overs in life.

"No, there was only Nando. He had a sweetheart named Maria, and we hoped for some little nietos by now. Grandchildren, I mean. She married another man a few weeks ago. Maria is a nice girl, and I hope she will be happy."

Again, Bowman didn't know what to say, but this time he said nothing. That was probably a good rule to follow. And then Bowman's food arrived, which jerked them both out of their private thoughts.

"Well, I must be getting back to work," said Mrs. Flores, rising from her seat and dabbing at her eyes with her napkin. After composing herself, she walked past him and out the door.

CHAPTER 14

"So I did what I could for him and started back here. It took me the rest of the night to get back. Deputy Abbott found me just outside of town."

Bowman was back at the Bronco County Sheriff's Department station house, but in a different room this time. This room had no mirror, and his leg wasn't shackled to the table. He wasn't a suspect this time, but a witness, and something of a hero. In the room with him were Sheriff Cane, Detectives Carrillo and Paine, and a young woman named Bates, a special agent with the Drug Enforcement Administration. Bates, rather than Carrillo, was asking the questions this time.

Bates wore no uniform, and was dressed in blue slacks and a white blouse, with her badge attached below her left shoulder. She carried a Glock 23 on her right hip. It was the compact version of the Glock, which made sense for her, because she was petite. Petite, but not fragile, with a lithe, athletic look, like a long-distance runner, and dark brown hair pulled back in a ponytail. Her most striking feature, however, was her green eyes. She was pretty, and she smelled nice.

She'd told him that a group of DEA agents had flown

in to the old mining camp, along with the medical helicopter. El Chato and his people were long gone, but DEA found plenty of evidence of their presence. And they found Walker. Just in time, they said. He hadn't yet regained consciousness, and it wasn't yet clear whether there would be any brain damage, but they'd been able to relieve the pressure on his brain in time to save his life, and the prognosis was good.

It was late afternoon when Agent Bates had arrived and asked Bowman to repeat what he'd told Abbott and Cane. She'd thanked him for all that he'd done for Walker, and had made it seem like a bigger deal than it actually was. What else could he have done? She pressed Bowman for details from time to time, but treated him respectfully, as a concerned citizen trying to help. Maybe more than respectfully. Or maybe that was wishful thinking on his part.

"You said that you didn't see what happened in the generator shed, is that correct?"

"Yes, ma'am. I mean, no, I did not see what happened."

"Please stop calling me ma'am. I'm no older than you are."

"I'm sorry," Bowman blurted out, feeling flustered and confused, "I didn't mean . . ." He saw that she was smiling, and he relaxed a little. "What should I call you?" He hoped she would give him her first name. He'd been wondering what it was.

"Agent Bates will do — for now."

For now? What did that mean? But before he could further consider that question, 'Agent Bates' continued her questioning.

"The two men that Agent Walker shot, are you certain that Walker shot first?"

Bowman was pretty sure that Walker had shot first, but he saw what Bates was trying to do. She was trying to make some room for an argument that what Walker had done was all done in self-defense. A little ambiguity was probably all that would be needed, since no prosecutor would have much appetite for prosecuting him in these circumstances. He didn't know if he would lie to protect Walker. He felt some sympathy for him, because of what had happened to his family, and he was invested in him in an odd way, having saved his life. But he didn't need to lie.

"No — Agent Bates — I'm not certain. As I said, it was all very confusing and chaotic. Men shouting, shots fired, those two fell. That's about all I know for sure."

Bowman could see the relief in her face. She'd taken a chance, and maybe hoped that he would play along. It would've backfired on her if he'd insisted that he was certain.

She handed him a card, and their fingers touched. Had she done that on purpose? She didn't seem to be in a hurry to pull her hand away, and he certainly wasn't.

Finally, she did pull her hand away, and said, "Thank you, Mr. Bowman. If you recall anything else that you think might be useful, or — if you have any questions, please call me."

Bowman looked at the card, which read 'Clementine Bates, Special Agent, United States Drug Enforcement Administration,' with a phone number and an email address. That's a pretty name, he thought, with a nineteenth-century ring to it. He wouldn't mind meeting her again, in different circumstances. He put the card in his pocket and tried to put those thoughts away. These were not different circumstances. He asked her, "Why was Walker out there by himself? Why didn't he call in some reinforcements?"

Clementine Bates considered before answering. Bowman figured that she was used to asking the questions, rather than answering them, and Bowman was just a witness, with no official capacity. But she must have decided that he was owed some answers, given what he'd been through, and she said, "Agent Walker wasn't on duty. He'd been put on leave, because of what happened to his family. We figured he needed the time off, and El Paso didn't want him working on this matter. He was too personally involved."

"So he went solo?"

"Looks like it," Bates said. "That old silver mine had been on our radar for a while, as a possible hideout for smugglers and such. We even flew over it a few times, but it looked unused from the air. It's not easy to get to on the ground. I don't know if Walker had some new information or just a hunch – I'll let Detective Paine fill you in on what he learned about that – but in any case he apparently decided to check it out. We found his truck about five miles west of the camp. Looks likes that's as far as he could get in his truck, and he hiked the rest of the way in. There's no phone reception out there, and he didn't have any radio equipment. When he found El Chato there, he should've come back for reinforcements. But I guess I understand why he didn't. He had a chance at the people who he believed had killed his family, and he took it. He couldn't know if they'd still be there when he got back with help."

"So what did you find at the camp, apart from Agent Walker?"

"They'd taken their own casualties away with them, but the blood stains and shell casings on the ground are consistent with what you told us. They had three SUVs, equipped for off-road travel, and we should be able to get some good castings of their tracks. We followed the tracks back to the road, a difficult and indirect route. They abandoned some supplies, what they didn't have room for or time to gather, I expect, but no useful documents. I'm pretty sure we'll find heroin residue. Maybe we'll get some fingerprints. I don't think they'll be going back." After a moment or two, she continued, "Oh yes, I almost forgot. We found these, which I think belong to you. Am I right?"

She handed him a plastic bag containing his extra clothes and his book.

"Thank you. How did you know they were mine?"

"Detective Carrillo told us that you were reading Moby Dick. We figured you'd want to finish it."

"Now that you've taken the trouble to fly it back to me on a helicopter, I guess I have to finish it."

"Yes," she said, smiling, "I would be very disappointed if you don't. And when you're done, maybe you'll lend it to me. It's been on my bucket list a long time."

Those beautiful green eyes light up when she smiles, Bowman thought, and felt his ears growing hot. Were they flirting? He'd never found it easy to talk to girls, and he felt the usual panic coming on. It was time to change the subject.

"I may have seen some of those men before," Bowman said. That got everyone's attention, and he continued, "Before I came into town the other day, I stopped at a little convenience store a few miles outside of town, with a cantina in the back. I didn't see a name on the place."

"I know the place," said Cane. "Gabe Leonard's place. Folks just call it Gabe's."

"There were four men at the cantina. They were dressed like some of the men I saw at the mining camp, and they drove a black SUV like the ones I saw at the camp. They tried to recruit me, but I passed."

"Recruit you for what?"

"They didn't say. I didn't let it get that far. But I assumed it was for some kind of security work. Looks like I was right."

"Can you describe them?" Clementine asked.

Bowman described them as well as he could, but found that, for most of them, it was difficult to get beyond approximate size, hair color and clothing, and he didn't think his descriptions would be very helpful. But the man he'd fought had made more of an impression.

"One of them took a swing at me, because I wouldn't have a beer with them. He was smaller than the others, with a narrow face and dark, deep-set eyes, like an angry weasel. And he'll probably have a big bruise on his face for the next few days."

"Because he took a swing at you?" Clementine asked, smiling. Those green eyes, again, Bowman thought, and had to force himself not to stare. He nodded, and she continued, "Did you get any names?"

"Just one. The one that seemed to be their leader, and did most of the talking, called himself Gordon."

Carrillo gave Bowman a disapproving look, and said, "Why did you not tell me this the other day, Mr. Bowman?"

"You didn't ask, Detective, and I was under arrest on suspicion of murder. I didn't want to admit to an assault, and I thought I should limit myself to answering direct questions. At the time I didn't see any connection to the murders."

Carrillo nodded, apparently satisfied with this explanation.

Bowman said, "They told me I could get in touch with them through the old man if I changed my mind. Maybe I should, so I can get close to El Chato and help you locate him."

Agent Clementine Bates was taken aback at first, but quickly said, "No, that's out of the question. You'd get yourself killed, and we can't be responsible for that. Leave this to the professionals, Mr. Bowman." After a moment she continued, in a softer tone, "It was very brave of you to suggest it, and I applaud your spirit, but we can't put a civilian into that kind of situation."

"Yeah, I guess it was a bad idea," Bowman said.

As everyone was getting ready to leave, Paine approached Bowman, looking a little sheepish.

"Listen, Bowman, I – uh . . ."

"Yes?" Bowman said. He no longer felt any ill will

towards Paine, who had just been doing his job, but he didn't think he needed to make this easy for him either.

"Well, you know, the other day . . ."

"You're sorry you were such a dick?"

"Yes, that's just the word I was looking for."

"Apology accepted."

They both smiled, but Bowman, and Paine, from the looks of it, felt awkward. After a few moments, Bowman continued, "Agent Bates said you had some ideas on why Walker suspected that El Chato was at that old mining camp."

"Yeah," said Paine, obviously relieved at the change of subject. "After the murders, Walker moved in with a friend of his. He'll probably never be able to sleep in his own house again." Paine frowned and shook his head, and then continued. "Anyway, while the DEA was checking out the camp, I went to where Walker was staying, to see if I could figure out why he'd gone out there. His friend hadn't seen him since the previous morning, but he told me that Walker had left a bunch of papers on the kitchen table, and he showed them to me. They were part of a file that Walker had been keeping on El Chato, including some aerial photos of that area."

"That doesn't really tell us why he thought El Chato might be there, does it?"

"No, it doesn't. Maybe he was grasping at straws, checking out all the possibilities he could think of. I don't know. But I think I do know why he thought that someone was at the mining camp."

"Something in the aerial photos?"

"Yes, but nothing that looked suspicious in any of the photos individually. The photos were taken over the course of months, and date stamped. He'd circled features in the photos that appeared to change from one photo to the next. Nothing dramatic, just a rut that hadn't been there before, a shadow that seemed longer, stuff like that."

"So he decided that someone was there, or had been

from time to time, and guessed that it was El Chato."

"Looks that way. He probably thought that it wasn't enough to convince the DEA to stage a raid, or maybe he wanted to do it on his own, with no interference and no witnesses. Can't say that I blame him, if that is what he was thinking. Anyway, you know the rest."

Paine left with Carrillo, and Bowman looked around the room for Clementine Bates. She was gone.

CHAPTER 15

Sheriff Cane let Bowman spend the night in the cell. Once again he was spared the bad dreams. He dreamed about Clementine Bates, but it wasn't a bad dream. It was an excellent dream. Maybe it had driven off the other dreams. He hoped they were gone for good, but suspected that they were not.

He was up and ready to go before Cane and Mrs. Flores arrived and relieved the deputy on the overnight shift. Mrs. Flores had brought donuts, which he guessed she did every day, and made a pot of coffee.

"Have a donut and a cup of coffee before you go, Robbie. I have packed a lunch for you. And I have brought some of Fernando's clothes that I thought might fit you. You can pick out what you want."

"Thank you, ma'am, that was very kind of you."

He felt a little strange going through Fernando's clothes, but could see that Mrs. Flores wanted him to, so be picked out a pair of socks, a pair of khaki pants and a gray long-sleeve shirt and put them in his pack.

"You know, you don't have to go right away, son," Sheriff Cane said. "Most folks know what you did by now, and you'd be welcome to stay. I'm sure we could find you

119

some work to do around town. This place is as good as anyplace else, I reckon."

Mrs. Flores visibly brightened at this prospect, and added, "You could stay in Nando's room until you found your own place!" Bowman thought that would be a terrible idea. It sounded way too much like trying to replace Fernando.

"Thank you, again, both of you. But I'm still looking for Bridget."

Mrs. Flores tried to hide her disappointment, but failed. Sheriff Cane looked like he knew all along what the answer would be. "Right. Your sister. Where you thinking of looking?"

"I don't know." Neither Cane nor Mrs. Flores said anything, and Bowman felt that he had to say more. "I can't stop looking just because I don't know where to look."

Cane looked like he wasn't persuaded of the sense of that statement, but after a few moments he said, "No, son, I don't reckon you can. Deputy Abbott is out on patrol, but he'll be back in a bit and can give you a ride out of town."

"Thanks, Sheriff, but I'll get started walking." Bowman gave them each a quick nod, shouldered his pack and headed out the door, eager to avoid any more awkward conversation. He decided to leave town the way he'd come in. Going west hadn't worked out well.

Outside, the morning was still cool, and he wanted to get some miles in before it got too hot. There was still some residual soreness here and there, but he'd pretty much recovered from his run through the desert, and he felt good.

As he walked, he considered what direction he should take once he reached the highway. Looking for Bridget didn't really limit his choices, since he had no idea where to look. Maybe Los Angeles. He suspected that L.A. got more than its share of runaways, with dreams of being 'discovered,' or just for the warm weather. He tried to remember if Bridget had ever talked about becoming a movie star, but nothing came to mind.

Or he could head to West Virginia and look up Clayton Boone's parents. But what purpose would it serve? Nothing he could tell them about how Boone died would be comforting, and it would probably just open some old wounds. Maybe he should just wait at the bus stop for the next bus and take it wherever it was going, rather than trying to hitch a ride one way or the other. That would relieve him of the decision, at least.

He was shocked out of his reverie three or four miles outside of town, when the black SUV came up from behind him and pulled alongside, on the other side of the road. Had they been following him?

Gordon, the one who had tried to recruit him a few days before, was driving, and Bowman's special friend was in the front passenger seat. He looked better than he had the last time Bowman had seen him, but a large yellowing bruise still covered most of his face. There was only one other man with them, in the back seat. He was one of the other two who had been at their first meeting.

"We heard you were picked up by the police," Gordon said. "Have some trouble with the law?" Gordon seemed friendly enough, but the man with the bruised face was stabbing at Bowman with his dark little eyes. These men were dangerous, he now knew, and he would need to be more careful in dealing with them than he'd been at their first meeting.

"Yeah," Bowman replied. "There was some trouble in town just after I arrived, and they thought I was involved. Eventually they figured out I wasn't and let me go." Bowman didn't know how much they knew, so he tried to be as vague as possible. He'd prefer them to think that he'd been held the entire time, so he wouldn't need to explain, or rather lie about, where he had been. But he didn't want to be caught in a lie.

Gordon nodded. "We heard about it. That was some nasty business. And a guy like you, with no job and no friends, is a natural target for the police. You must have had a lot of time to think about your situation, over that last couple of days. Given any more thought to my proposal?"

Bowman had put the idea of infiltrating El Chato's organization out of his head after Bates had rejected it so forcefully. He wasn't a cop, and this wasn't his problem. But he'd changed his mind as soon as the black SUV had pulled up to him. All of these things coming together as they had must mean something. He didn't believe that some old man with a long white beard was sitting on a cloud and manipulating a set of strings, but he had a sense that he was meant to get involved. Call it fate. He wasn't eager – in fact, he was highly reluctant – but he knew that only he had this opportunity to get close to the murderers, and only he could take it.

"Maybe," Bowman said. "I could use some extra cash, and I don't have anything else going on." He concentrated on trying to keep the nervousness out of his voice and manner.

"Then happening upon you like this was a happy coincidence for both of us. Jump in."

Bowman doubted that they'd just happened upon him, but he let that pass. From the sound of it, they hadn't heard about Bowman's new status in town. He hoped they wouldn't. If they did, his status with them would instantly change from new recruit to potential witness for the prosecution. He wasn't ready to jump in just yet.

"I have a few questions first. To start with, who would I be working for, and what would I be doing?" Bowman didn't want to come across as too curious, but he didn't want to appear too eager either. No one would sign up with this group without asking a few questions. He'd have to walk a fine line.

"We provide private security. You would be working

under me, with my two colleagues here. I'm sure you remember Hawk," he said, and motioned with his head towards the man with the bruised face, with what Bowman was pretty sure was a wink. He looks like a hawk, thought Bowman, with that narrow face, sharp nose and those little eyes, and the yellowing bruise adds to the resemblance. "The guy in the back calls himself Sanborn. Our boss is a Mexican guy. I don't know his real name, and he doesn't know ours. We don't need to know your real name, either. Just tell us what you want us to call you."

"I don't speak Spanish. Does your boss speak English?"

"Not much. But don't worry about that. I speak Spanish and will do all the talking."

"I assume your boss is involved in something illegal," Bowman said. "That isn't necessarily a deal breaker, but there are different kinds of illegal."

"Assume whatever you want, but your life will be a lot easier if you stick to your own business and don't ask questions." Gordon's tone had hardened somewhat, and Bowman was intensely aware of the precariousness of his situation. If this conversation went badly it could be his last. But now was not the time to show fear or appear timid.

"Only an idiot would sign up blind for something like this," he said. From the look on Sanborn's face, he guessed that Sanborn had done exactly that. "You don't want someone who's gonna have second thoughts after figuring out what's going on."

Gordon did not reply for some time, but just looked at Bowman with an unreadable expression. He began to wonder whether he'd overplayed his hand.

Finally, Gordon said, "The boss buys and sells — controlled substances. He has connections in Mexico for his source, and he distributes the — product — in the U.S." Gordon must have felt the need to justify being involved with that, for he continued, "He satisfies demand for a product that people choose to buy of their own free will. I never touch any of that stuff myself, but that's just me. If somebody wants to use it, who am I to say they can't? It doesn't hurt anyone else."

Bowman thought of Fernando Flores. Perhaps he had made his own choices, but he wasn't the only one hurt by those choices. But this wasn't the time for a philosophical argument.

"So who does your boss need protection from?"

"The people he buys from and the people he sells to, mostly, and maybe potential competitors. He does business with some very bad people, people who might be tempted to kill him so they can keep the cash and the merchandise. We are on hand to make sure that doesn't happen. He's no saint, but the people we protect him from are no better, maybe worse. And he pays us well."

"And how much does he pay?" Bowman asked. It seemed like the obvious question.

"For you, a thousand dollars a week, in cash. After a while, if you work out, it may be more. And sometimes there are bonuses for a job well done." Behind Gordon, Bowman saw Hawk smirk at the mention of bonuses.

"What about your friend there, Hawk? Is he going to be OK with me?"

Gordon turned to Hawk and said, "Please tell our new friend here that you've already forgotten the little schoolyard scrap you two indulged in, and that you're ready to restart your relationship with a clean slate."

Hawk's unfriendly expression did not change, but he said, "Sure. Clean slate."

"There you go," Gordon said, turning back to Bowman. "Satisfied?"

He was not satisfied, but he was not going to walk away now.

"Last time I saw you there were four of you. Why isn't the fourth guy with you now?"

Bowman saw that Gordon was a little rattled by the

question, and he took a few moments to reply. Would he lie?

"He's dead. That's a risk we take, of course, and why the pay is so good. Usually just a show of force is all that's needed, and we rarely have to fire our weapons. But the other night some crazy bastard attacked us, and killed Ford and a couple of others. I don't know who he was or why he attacked us. The boss seemed to know, but he didn't say and I didn't ask."

"So what happened to the crazy bastard?"

Gordon seemed reluctant to answer the question, but after a moment he said, "He was killed."

So they hadn't heard. This might work.

Hawk smirked again, and Bowman felt an almost overpowering urge to smash that yellow face again. There was a long, awkward silence, which Bowman finally broke.

"OK, I'm in. You can call me Archer."

CHAPTER 16

"You can take the blindfold off now," Gordon said, as he opened the door of the SUV.

Bowman did so, stepped out of the SUV and blinked in the late afternoon light. Once his eyes had adjusted, he looked around to get his bearings. They'd driven to this place over a long dirt track, and must be at least a couple of miles from the paved road. On the way in, they'd lurched into and out of several dry washes, and had never gone in a straight line for long, so Bowman knew that it was little more than a track.

This place looked like it had been a working ranch once, but he saw no horses or cattle now. At the near end of the dirt track was an arched entranceway of gray, weathered wood that they'd just driven through. At one time, the arch had spelled out the name of the ranch in wooden letters, but most of the letters had fallen off. He was looking back at the arch, so he was on the wrong side to read it easily, but he could tell that the name was no longer decipherable. The letters on either end of the arch had fared best. He could make out the 'Th' at the beginning and the 'anch' at the end. In the middle of the arch however, only two letters remained, a 'c' and an 'n' a few spaces apart, both of which were hanging askew.

A little past the arch and to the left, coming in, was the ranch house, which faced to the right. It was a single level, with a long porch, or ramada, running along its entire front. The wooden floor of the ramada was just above ground level, and there was no railing. To the right, opposite the ranch house, was a long, low building, side on to the dusty courtyard between it and the ranch house. It faced a larger building that looked like a barn, about fifty yards back from the gate. To the left of the barn was an empty corral, enclosed by wooden rails. A well stood in the courtyard, more or less in the middle of the group of buildings. All of the buildings and the rails around the corral were of the same gray, weathered wood. Bowman could hear the low hum of a generator, and could see power lines running from the barn to the ranch house and the bunkhouse. He counted three American guards, all dressed and equipped like those at the old mining camp.

After Bowman had gotten into the SUV, Gordon had told him that he would need a haircut and some new clothes, and they'd driven to a small town about twenty minutes away. Hawk and Sanborn had said nothing, but were clearly studying Bowman. They'd dropped him off at a barbershop and Gordon had given him twenty dollars and said he would pick him up in half an hour. Bowman had reached for his pack.

"Leave that with us, Archer, if you don't mind. I'll need to look through it," Gordon said. "I won't take anything."

"Of course," Bowman said, trying not to sound as tense as he felt. He knew he should've expected that, but he hadn't. Was there anything in his pack that would betray him? He didn't think so. Agent Bates had rejected his plan, so she hadn't offered him any kind of wire or tracking device. He relaxed a little.

Bowman got the same haircut as Gordon and the others. He was the only customer, and the barber wasn't chatty. Bowman was grateful for that, because he wanted to think. Had he just made a huge mistake? There was still time to back out. The murders of Walker's wife and their little girl, and the shooting of Walker himself, had been horrific, but it wasn't his responsibility to avenge them. He was just passing through. What did any of this have to do with him? But he felt that it was his responsibility, although he couldn't say quite why. To atone for all his sins, mortal and venal? Because only he had this chance to get close to the murderers? Because he had nothing else to do and was looking for some excitement? All of the above?

They picked him up outside the barbershop and drove out of town. Gordon said, "We picked you up some new clothes, so you'll look the part. We don't wear uniforms, but the boss wants us to look professional. I put them in your pack." Bowman said nothing, and Gordon continued, "I see you're reading Moby Dick. I started it once, but couldn't finish it. I didn't need to know that much about whaling."

"Maybe he got paid by the word. I'll let you know if it picks up at all towards the end," Bowman said.

"What is that, a book?" said Sanborn.

"Yes, Sanborn," Gordon said, "it's a very obscure book about a white whale and a guy with a peg leg. I'm not surprised you've never heard of it." Bowman smiled. He was beginning to like Gordon, despite the circumstances. To Bowman, Gordon said, "That's a nice knife you have. Were you Special Forces?"

"No, I had to buy mine."

Gordon nodded. Bowman suspected that Gordon already knew that. The versions issued to the Special Forces were labeled "Yarborough," and each had a unique serial number. Gordon must know that, because he'd recognized the knife, and would've looked at the blade. Was Gordon testing him, to see if he would claim to be Special Forces? Had he been Special Forces himself?

Bowman was faintly ashamed that all of these men were ex-military, like him, and that shame led to anger. He felt that what they were doing, who they were working for, reflected badly on him and his brothers-in-arms. And the Special Forces were the elite, so that sense of betrayal was intensified. He would have to suppress that anger, though, at least for now.

Once they were past the last of the houses of the town, Gordon pulled over to the side of the road and said, "We're going to have to search you and blindfold you before we go any further. The boss has a lot of enemies, and we need to be careful. You can back out now, and we'll drop you off here with a free haircut and some new clothes. If you come with us, you won't be able to come and go as you please. You can leave, of course, but you won't be able to choose the time and place. You still in?"

Bowman wondered why Gordon was giving him so many chances to back out. Gordon would not want someone on his team who wasn't fully committed, but Bowman sensed that it was more than that. Gordon had approached him, and he seemed to like Bowman, but now Gordon seemed almost reluctant to accept him. Should he take the hint and back out while he still could? A few moments passed as he hesitated under their watchful gaze.

"I'm in," he said at last, and they patted him down, blindfolded him and drove to the ranch. He felt intensely vulnerable; he was unarmed, blindfolded and trapped in an SUV with three armed drug traffickers, at least one of whom actively hated him. It would be easy for them to kill him and dump his body in the desert. When he was finally allowed to remove his blindfold the relief was immense, even though he knew that the danger hadn't abated by much.

"Wait here," Gordon said, and walked up to the ranch house door and knocked. In a few moments, the door was opened and Gordon spoke in Spanish to someone inside. Soon El Chato himself appeared on the ramada, along with two other Mexican men. Bowman recognized him from the mining camp. He'd been at some distance, and it had been dark, but there was no mistaking the short, solid form and the dark, flat face, nor, especially, the way he carried himself. It left no doubt who was in charge.

All three Mexicans wore short sleeved, button-front white shirts over dark pants. All three had pistols, also, and the two other men carried rifles as well, slung across the front. One of the rifles looked like an M4 carbine. The other was a Heckler and Koch UMP9, a compact submachine gun. Bowman had seen pictures of the UMP9 in the Soldier of Fortune magazines that were always left lying around military bases, but this was the first time he'd seen one in person.

El Chato spoke with Gordon in Spanish. Bowman couldn't hear what was said, and would not have understood much anyway, but they looked over at him from time to time, and he presumed that they were talking about him.

After a few minutes, El Chato walked over to Bowman, leaving Gordon back with the other two Mexicans. He stopped just in front of Bowman, close enough to be intimidating, which it was, but far enough so that he did not need to look up at Bowman. He said nothing, just studied Bowman with an impassive expression. El Chato's face could have been carved from walnut, and his black eyes revealed nothing of his soul, leaving Bowman with the unnerving feeling that he had none. He remembered watching this man shoot the helpless Walker without hesitation, and knew that El Chato would kill him just as summarily if he guessed his intentions. Bowman concentrated on keeping those intentions from showing in his face.

Finally, to Bowman's relief, he turned and walked back towards Gordon and the others. Without stopping, he nodded at Gordon and went back inside, followed by the other two men. Gordon walked back to the SUV.

"OK, Archer, your appointment has been confirmed. Grab your bag and follow me. You too, Sanborn." Turning to Hawk, he said, "Park the truck and then join us in the bunkhouse." Then he headed towards the building on the right, followed by Bowman and Sanborn.

"You sure he's going to be OK with me?" Bowman asked Gordon, nodding his head in the direction of the SUV, which Hawk was driving towards the barn. "It looks like he hasn't forgiven me yet for the facial reconstruction."

Gordon chuckled. "I wouldn't turn my back on him if I were you, but I think he'll be wary of you from now on. You don't have to be friends, and if you were you'd probably be the first friend he ever had."

That's a good sign, Bowman thought. They recognize that there's something off with Hawk. What could fill a man with hate like that? Bowman was the current focus of Hawk's hate, but he figured that it had been there for a long time. But the reason didn't matter now; you had to take a man as you found him.

The bunkhouse looked like it could've housed twenty or thirty cowboys, in double-decker bunk beds. But the bunk beds were missing the mattresses and were all pushed up against the sides of the bunkhouse, in various stages of decay. In the cleared space there were eight cots, four on each side of the door, and a couple of weapon racks.

"These four bunks to the right of the door here are ours," Gordon said. "Yours is the one on the far end. The bunks on the other side belong to the other unit. We're Alpha Squad, they're Bravo. Bravo is on duty at the moment. Put on those clothes I bought you and we'll pick out some weapons for you."

Bowman put his pack on his cot and pulled out the clothes, a pair of khaki cargo pants, a web belt and a dark green twill shirt. He put them on, along with his own boots and boonie hat, and put the clothes he'd been wearing in his pack. Then he took out his knife and threaded the web belt through the sheath to secure it on his left hip. His right hip was reserved for his pistol. Gordon noticed, and nodded.

"I have one just like it," Gordon said, and held up his own, which he'd pulled from a bag at the foot of his cot. It was in its sheath, but Bowman suspected that the blade would be inscribed with the name "Yarborough" and a serial number. Gordon nodded towards the weapons rack on their side of the bunkhouse and said, "Take your pick from those on the right. The ones on the left are taken."

The choice of long arms was limited to a shotgun and a civilian version of the M4 carbine. The civilian version of the M4 was semi-automatic only, so it couldn't fire three-round bursts like the military version. It had a shorter barrel than the M16, and a telescoping stock, so it was easier to carry in vehicles and other confined spaces, but fired the same 5.56 millimeter round. The main trade-off was less accuracy at longer distances. But most firefights happened at ranges of no more than a couple hundred yards, and at that distance the M4 was accurate enough. The other choice was a Mossberg pump-action twelve-gauge shotgun. It was great for close quarters fighting, like clearing buildings, but Bowman preferred the M4 for most situations. It was more accurate and held more rounds. Bowman hoped that he wouldn't need to fire his weapon, but if he did he might want to miss his apparent target, and it was hard to miss with the shotgun without being obvious. He chose the M4 and a full thirty-round magazine.

Slotting the magazine in place and patting the side of the M4, he said to Gordon, "Like an old friend I never thought I'd see again."

Gordon smiled. "When you really need a friend, there is none better."

The choices for side arms were the Glock 17 and the Beretta 92, both semi-automatic pistols that fired a nine-millimeter round. The Glock had a seventeen-round magazine, while the Beretta's magazine held fifteen rounds. Bowman was most familiar with the Beretta 92, which was standard Army issue, as the M9, but he'd fired the Glock 17 on occasion. He chose the Beretta, primarily because it had a more solid feel to it that he liked, being composed of more metal and less polymer. Two fewer rounds in the magazine wasn't likely ever to be an issue, he thought.

Gordon took an M4 and a Beretta from the guns on the left, and Sanborn took a shotgun and a Glock. Bowman hadn't wanted the shotgun for himself, but thought it was a good idea to have one in the squad, for flexibility.

By the time Bowman had chosen his weapons, Hawk had returned from parking the SUV. He rummaged in a bag at the foot of his cot and produced a black tactical tomahawk, which he slung in its sheath under his left arm, with the handle hanging down. Bowman had seen versions of the tactical tomahawk before, primarily in Afghanistan. It was a modern version of the classic American Indian weapon, with a stainless steel head and a composite handle. In addition to an axe blade that was as long as Bowman's knife blade, there was a secondary spear point on the back side of the head. They were not military issue, and anyone who wanted one had to buy it, as he had bought his Green Beret Knife. He'd considered buying one, before he decided on the knife. A tomahawk had some advantages, if there was enough room to maneuver. It had a longer reach, and a man could generate more force swinging a tomahawk than he could thrusting or slashing with a knife. And it looked formidable. But resorting to your blade was usually a last, desperate measure, and you were more likely to be rolling on the ground with your enemy than circling him on open ground. In close quarters, the knife would be easier to use. He'd been right too, the one time it had mattered.

Bowman wondered whether the tomahawk was the source of Hawk's nickname. It seemed more plausible than his hawk-like face, if he'd chosen it himself.

Hawk saw Bowman looking at the tomahawk and grinned, but with his mouth only; his eyes still spat hate at Bowman. "Maybe we should see which is more effective one of these days," he said, looking at Bowman's knife.

"That sounds like great fun," Bowman said dryly, "I'll try to make room in my schedule." But it didn't sound like fun at all. In an arranged duel, with plenty of room to maneuver, the tomahawk would have all the advantages.

"That's enough bickering, children," Gordon said irritably. "We need to relieve Bravo Squad."

Hawk took the last of the weapons on the left, an M4 and a Glock, and they all walked out of the bunkhouse.

"Hawk, you relieve Samson. Sanborn, you relieve Carter. Archer and I will take over from Blake." Blake was apparently the guard stationed in the area between the barn and the ranch house, because Gordon started in that direction, and Bowman followed. Hawk was moving towards the area by the entrance, between the bunkhouse and the ranch house, while Sanborn was headed towards the area between the barn and the bunkhouse. Those three positions covered all approaches to the ranch.

As they neared him, Blake came forward and said, "You sure took your time, Gordon. Where the hell you been? And who's this guy?" Blake carried a scoped, bolt-action hunting rifle with a black composite stock. A 30-06, Bowman thought. It must be the one he'd seen at the mining camp. For covering open terrain like that around the ranch, it was a good choice.

"I've been recruiting, Blake. This is Archer. He'll be sticking close to me for a while, until he gets a little more settled in."

That seemed to assuage Blake's irritation, and he said, "We could use the extra help now, for sure." He nodded at Bowman, wiped the sweat from his brow with his shirt sleeve and walked away towards the bunkhouse.

Bowman looked around. They were at the back left corner of the barn, between it and the corral. The bunkhouse was screened from their view by the barn, but they could see the side of the ranch house and all approaches to the ranch for almost one hundred eighty degrees. Bowman had seen that Hawk and Sanborn could each observe a similar portion of the approaches. There was substantial overlap, but there were areas that only one of them could watch. The area surrounding the ranch was much like what he'd traversed the other day, mostly flat desert landscape, with patches of cactus, yucca and desert grasses scattered around, cut here and there by dry washes. Bowman wondered how a ranch could've survived in an area like this, with so little water and grass. Maybe it hadn't always been so dry.

After a few minutes, he said to Gordon, "So what's the routine, apart from what we're doing right now?"

Gordon glanced at Bowman briefly, and then continued to scan the horizon as he spoke. "Well, we, by which I mean Alpha and Bravo Squads, provide perimeter security, and security for transactions. Perimeter security is taken much more seriously since the attack the other day. We're all Americans and, I think, all ex-military. We mostly don't share a lot of personal history, and I recommend the same for you. I, for one, will not be coming back for any reunions."

Gordon doesn't seem happy to be here, thought Bowman. So why was he here? And what about the others? Where they all as ambivalent as Gordon?

"What about the two guys who were with the boss? They didn't look like Americans."

"No, they're both Mexican, like the boss. The boss is called El Chato, a nickname. The other two are Paco and Esteban. They've been with him since way back, before I got involved. There used to be another one, named Pedro, but he got killed with Ford and Stokes. Ford was in our squad, Stokes was in Bravo." Gordon looked down and kicked absent mindedly at a clod of dirt before continuing. "Anyway, they stick close to Chato, and we don't have to deal with them much. Blake runs Bravo, and I deal with Chato on behalf of both squads. You shouldn't have to deal with any of them, and I recommend that you don't."

Was Gordon trying to protect him, or just ensure his control by limiting access to the boss?

"Did those three guys get killed here at this ranch?" Bowman asked, feigning ignorance.

Bowman reflected that the high mortality rate in this job would've bothered him a lot more if he hadn't known the reason for it, but he didn't think something like the attack by Walker was likely to happen again.

"No, that was at a different place, and I don't think we'll be going back there. Chato has a few places, and we move around a lot." He was silent for a while, and then said, "Jesus, that didn't make any sense to me. The guy was all by himself, and attacked us. He cut Pedro's throat, and Ford and Stokes were killed in a firefight that followed. I don't miss Pedro – he was a nasty one – but Ford and Stokes were all right. I can't imagine what the guy was thinking."

Bowman was glad to hear that Gordon and the other Americans hadn't known who Walker was. All they knew was that they were attacked and they defended themselves. Perhaps they were not too far gone to be turned back on the right path. The easiest way to bring El Chato down might be to turn his own security team against him. If Bowman was going to do that, Gordon would be the place to start. But he needed a better feel for the situation before he made any move.

"You said earlier that El Chato seemed to know who he was," Bowman said.

"He did. I think he said the guy's name was Walker, or something like that. My guess is he was looking for revenge for something Chato had done to him, something personal. A man doesn't go on a suicide mission like that because he was cheated in a drug deal. But Chato didn't say, and I didn't ask. The less we know about what he does the better, I think."

So your excuse is ignorance, thought Bowman, but it's willful ignorance. At the appropriate time, he would need to deprive them of that excuse by telling Gordon and the other Americans the full story, or as much as he knew of it.

"So Walker, or whatever his name was, was killed in the firefight?" Bowman asked, trying to sound only mildly curious.

Gordon didn't answer for a long time, looking off into the desert. Finally, he said, "Yeah."

Gordon and Bowman lapsed into silence. Bowman had more questions, but he felt that he was pushing his luck already. It would not do to appear too curious.

Soon the sun set in a wash of red and orange, and the stars came out. The moon was waning and would not rise for some time, allowing the stars to dominate the night sky. This was what Bowman loved best about the desert. In the dry air, far from the light of towns and cities, the Milky Way and the constellations came alive, and Bowman felt a connection with all those who had lived before electric lights had nearly cut us off from the heavens. From early man trekking across the African savanna to cowboys following their herds, we had all looked up at the same sky and, Bowman presumed, felt the same sense of limitless grandeur. Those of us who were cut off from that by the overpowering glow of modern life were missing something vital.

Reluctantly, Bowman shook himself out of his reverie and considered his situation. The reason he'd joined Gordon was to find out where El Chato was hiding and get that information to Clementine Bates or Sheriff Cane. He'd found El Chato, but he had no way of communicating with them, and even if he had, he didn't know where he was. And he was now involved with some dangerous people, who would not hesitate to kill him if they suspected what he was up to. Hawk already wanted to kill him. Gordon seemed like a decent man who had made some bad decisions, and maybe some of the others were as well, but they worked for El Chato now and he had to assume that they'd follow his orders. He could expect no help from Bates or Cane, who didn't even know what he was doing. All he could do was play the role he'd assumed and look for opportunities. If he could win the support of the American security team, perhaps they could arrest El Chato themselves, although the chances of being able to do that without someone getting killed appeared to be slim. It would be easier and safer to kill El Chato and his Mexicans without any preliminaries, if he could win over the Americans, but Bowman would not go down that road. He would not pretend, even to himself, that he wasn't capable of murder. Anyone was, he thought, if pushed hard enough, as hard as Walker had been, perhaps. But he hadn't yet reached that point, and he hoped he never would.

CHAPTER 17

"Drop your cocks and pick up your socks, my friends," said Gordon, banging a serving spoon against a frying pan as he walked along the line of cots. "Turn out and suit up for transaction security."

Bravo Squad had relieved them a couple of hours before dawn. Someone had brought a big pan of scrambled eggs and toast from the ranch house, which they ate before hitting their cots for a few hours of sleep. It was now about mid-day.

"Bravo will stay behind and Alpha Squad will have the honor of accompanying the boss and his compatriots to the transaction site. Time to earn your pay, Archer."

"Shit," Sanborn said. "I just fell asleep."

"No rest for the weary, I'm afraid. Hop to, my friends. Chato and his crew are waiting for us."

Bowman groaned and swung his legs over the edge of his cot, then stood up and rummaged around for his clothes. They were all soon dressed and equipped, and headed out of the bunkhouse as a group.

They were in the barn, preparing to board the SUV, when Bowman's eye caught sight of something amid a pile of rusting equipment against the wall, just a few feet from where he stood next to the SUV's front passenger door. It was a metal rod about two and a half feet long, shaped into a triangular handle on one end and attached to some kind of design of metal on the other. It was a branding iron, he realized. Gordon was already in the driver's seat, and Sanborn was climbing into the rear seat, behind Gordon.

"Come on, Archer, get in," Gordon said. "They're waiting for us."

"One sec, I just want to have a look at this," Bowman said. He stepped over to the wall, grabbed the branding iron and quickly returned and climbed into the SUV across from Gordon.

"Whatcha got there?" Gordon asked, looking over at the length of rusty iron.

"Not sure," Bowman answered. "I think it's a branding iron. I've never seen one of these, outside of the movies. I didn't think they still used these."

"Maybe they don't. That one looks like it hasn't been used in a while."

Gordon backed out of the barn and then drove the short distance to line up behind the SUV parked in front of the ranch house, which contained El Chato, Paco and Esteban. Paco was driving and Esteban was in the back. El Chato's SUV pulled away and Gordon followed it through the arch and down the long approach road.

Bowman examined the brand as they drove down the dirt track. Part of it looked like old-fashioned football goal posts, or a capital letter "H." Bowman didn't think that a rancher would try to represent goal posts in his brand, and presumed that it was meant to be an H. Above or below the H – he couldn't tell which end the top was – there was a semicircle. So it was an H with a rounded hat, or an H in a bowl, or maybe a smiling H. Had this place once been known as the Hatted H Ranch, or the Smiling H Ranch? Neither one sounded likely. Bowman thought of asking Gordon, but decided that it would betray too much curiosity. They'd blindfolded him before bringing him here, so it was clear that they didn't want him to know where he was. If he had a chance to communicate with Clementine Bates or Sheriff Cane, he could describe the brand, and maybe they could determine where he was from that. And he would pay attention to where they were going now. Maybe he would see some kind of landmark that could be used to determine where he was.

Hawk had not been in the bunkhouse when Gordon had woken them. Bowman had thought that he must have been somewhere nearby, but he hadn't come with them.

"Hawk's not coming with us?" Bowman asked Gordon.

"No. Chato sent him on some errand."

"You mean you sent him on some errand for Chato? Don't you run the security team?"

The question seemed to annoy Gordon, or remind him of something that annoyed him. "No, Chato talks directly to Hawk, and gives him special jobs from time to time. I don't like it. It's not good for unit discipline, and Hawk gets an attitude from time to time, implying he could go over my head if he wanted to. On the other hand, I'm not sure I'd want to be in that chain of command. Whatever he has Hawk doing, he doesn't want me to know about it, and I'd just as soon not know."

Sanborn had been quiet up till then, but spoke now, saying, "I kind of like not having him around, actually, even if we have to take up the slack." Gordon said nothing in reply, but nodded in silent agreement.

They drove for about an hour, over back roads through the same desert terrain. They passed a few isolated houses or geographic features that Bowman thought he would recognize if he saw them again, but he saw nothing that he could use as a landmark for someone else to locate the ranch. Eventually, they came to a crossroads of a sort, though neither road was more than a pair of tire tracks. On the far side of the crossroads, waiting for them, were two vehicles, a blue extended cab pickup truck and a metallic gray SUV, parked one behind the other. El Chato's vehicle stopped just short of the crossroads, on the right, and Gordon pulled over on the left side of the road and a little behind it. This gave them a view of the two other vehicles, unobstructed by El Chato's SUV. For a minute or two, everyone remained in their vehicles. Then the doors of the other two vehicles swung open and eight men stepped out, four from each. All were armed, but they didn't look as professional as El Chato's group. They carried a wide variety of weapons, from shotguns to hunting rifles, and apparently had no dress code. Some looked like bikers, with long hair and beards, leather vests and heavy boots. Others looked like Bowman's conception of Ozark moonshiners, in jeans, sleeveless flannel shirts and caps that advertised some kind of seed corn. But all of them looked like violent men.

Gordon's M4 had been at Bowman's feet while Gordon was driving, and Bowman passed it to him now. "Just follow my lead," Gordon said, as he opened his door and climbed out. He stood just to the left of his open door, with his M4 held in front of him, pointing down and to his left. Bowman did the same on his side, and saw that Sanborn did the same behind Gordon, but only after he'd opened the right-side passenger door. Bowman guessed that the idea was to suggest that there were four of them, rather than three. After Alpha Squad was in position, El Chato, Paco and Esteban emerged from their vehicle, Esteban holding a small beige case. Once again, no one moved for a few moments. If this was an ambush, now would be the time to open fire. Bowman tightened his grip on his rifle and blinked sweat from his eyes.

One of the moonshiners seemed to be taking a particular interest in Bowman, fixing him with an arrogant stare. He was a big man, with broad shoulders, thickly muscled arms and a narrow waist. This one wasn't advertising any seed corn, and his unruly black hair was free and unencumbered. Li'l Abner with a bad attitude.

He held a double-barreled shotgun in his right hand, the stock pointing at the ground in front of him, the barrel resting on his shoulder. His left thumb was hooked in a belt loop. From time to time, without turning his head or taking his eyes from Bowman, he would send a stream of tobacco juice off to his side, first to the right, then to the left.

Bowman wasn't going to be drawn into some kind of macho staring match, and he continued scanning the group as a whole. A professional doesn't let his ego lead him around by the nose. If it didn't go beyond staring, Li'l Abner could have his little victory.

It apparently was not an ambush, because three of the men from the gray SUV on the other side of the crossroads started walking towards the middle of the crossroads. The protocol seemed to require the buyers to always move first. A moment later, El Chato, Paco and Esteban started walking to the same spot. One of the three other men, one of the bikers, carried a black satchel. As soon as the two groups met, the biker handed the satchel to El Chato, who opened it and examined the contents. Bowman could see that the satchel contained cash, because El Chato pulled out one banded bundle and examined it more closely, flipping through it and pulling out a bill at random to hold up to the light. He was apparently satisfied, because he nodded to Esteban, who passed the beige case over to one of the other three.

This man, the best dressed of the group, wore tan slacks, a pale blue blazer over a white shirt with an open collar, and a panama hat. He opened the case and quickly looked through it. Then he pulled out a small pen knife and cut open one of the packages inside. He wet a finger on his tongue and used it to taste some of the merchandise.

After nothing more than a quick nod, he closed the case and walked back to their corner, followed by the other two, as El Chato's group walked back to theirs. Li'l

Abner was the last of the buyers' group to get back in his vehicle, giving Bowman one last contemptuous look and sending one last stream of tobacco juice into the dust. No doubt Daisy Mae would hear the story of how he'd stared down the big bad soldier boy.

Gordon and the rest of Alpha Squad remained in position until the other vehicles had turned around and headed back in the direction from which they'd come. After the Americans were back aboard, El Chato's SUV turned around and headed back the way they'd come, and Gordon followed. The entire transaction had taken less than five minutes.

After a few minutes, Bowman asked Gordon, "Are they always that easy?"

"I've never had one blow up on me," Gordon replied. "Sometimes there's a little bluster or tension, arguments about quantity or quality or whatever, but we've never had to fire our weapons. This time Chato was selling, and the buyers tend to be less professional and more nervous than the sellers. You'll see when we cover a buy transaction. Those guys are almost all Mexicans, cartel members I'd guess, and they are not to be messed with. They've got all the best equipment, and they look like they know how to use it. But they are also very cool, and you know they won't panic and do something stupid. So I think these sell transactions are more likely to go bad, but we're also more likely to survive if one does. Pick your poison, I guess."

They drove on in silence for a while. The day was getting hot, and the landscape shimmered from the distortion caused by the superheated air. Tall cacti in the distance seemed to shimmy like belly dancers, with arms raised and hips swaying. Bowman thought about Clementine Bates. He'd like to see her again, after this was all over, but he didn't think he would ever work up the courage to call her. What could he possibly say? And what would she see in him? An unemployed drifter, that's what. She could probably have her pick of men, men with jobs and places to live. No, it wasn't going to happen. Better get back to planet Earth.

"How often do we do these?" Bowman asked. "These transactions, I mean."

Gordon glanced over at Bowman. "Well, it varies, but the sell transactions are much more common than the buy transactions. The buys are maybe once every month or two. We did one of those just a couple of days ago, so we won't be doing another for some time."

"Thank God," interjected Sanborn, from the back seat. "I still have the willies from that last one."

"Yeah," agreed Gordon, "the buys can be scary, but at least they're not as frequent. We do sell transactions every few days. Sometimes a whole week goes by between sales, and occasionally we'll do a couple in the same day. Like I said, it varies."

No one said anything more for several minutes, until Gordon suddenly said, "Oh shit!"

Bowman saw that Gordon was looking in the rear view mirror, and he checked the side mirror. There was a police car behind them, with its overhead lights on, another of those Explorer SUVs. Ahead of them, El Chato's SUV had pulled over to the side of the road, and Gordon pulled over behind him. The police car pulled over about ten yards behind them. The cop didn't get out of his car immediately, and it looked to Bowman like he was speaking on his radio.

"What do we do?" Sanborn said, panic in his voice.

Good question, thought Bowman. His plan had been to bring the police to El Chato, but not like this. This would not end well.

Gordon's knuckles were white on the steering wheel, and his face was pale and taut. He was clearly focused on the same question as Sanborn. Finally, he said, "Drop your weapons on the floor, keep your hands visible and do as ordered. We're not killing any cops for El Chato."

Bowman put his M4 down at his feet, next to

Gordon's, did the same with his Beretta and his knife, and then put his hands on the dashboard in front of him. This was going better than he'd expected, so far. Bowman sensed that Sanborn could've gone either way on the question of what to do about the cop, but was happy to do as he was told. He was glad that Hawk wasn't with them. Bowman wasn't particularly worried about being caught with El Chato; he could explain why he was there, and he thought he would be believed. But a lot of other things could go wrong.

Bowman watched in the side mirror as the cop climbed out of his cruiser and started walking towards Gordon's door, his hand on his holstered gun. It was Abbott. Ken Abbott. Young, earnest, naïve. Walking into a shit storm. Or maybe not. Gordon, at least, was standing down. Maybe this would work out.

Gordon lowered his window and put his hands on the steering wheel, at ten and two o'clock. As soon as Abbott reached the open window, he could see the weapons at Bowman's feet, and he quickly stepped back a pace, pulled his gun and leveled it.

"Keep your hands where I can see them and get out of the car, all of you!" he shouted, moving his gun around to try to cover all three them at once. He glanced quickly to his left, at El Chato's SUV, seemingly unsure of how to handle this situation. The windows were tinted, and he couldn't see who or what was in the front SUV. But it hardly mattered just then, because he had no choice now but to secure the men in the rear SUV before deciding what to do about the front one.

Bowman wanted to back him up somehow, but if he stepped out of the car with a weapon now he would be shot, and deserve to be. He would try to get Abbott settled first, then he could switch sides, if Abbott was willing to trust him.

Gordon, Sanborn and Bowman began to climb out of their SUV, moving slowly and keeping their hands visible as much as possible. Abbott moved a couple of paces back, towards the middle of the road, to create some space between him and the two nearer men, Gordon and Sanborn. "Turn around and put your hands on the roof of the car," he said. The tension was evident in his voice and manner, but he wasn't panicking. He was in control and focused. As the first two men complied he turned to the third, Bowman.

The shock was apparent on Abbott's face, and his eyes widened as he shouted, "You! What the hell are you . . ." He never finished what he was about to say, because just then he saw something out of the corner of his eye and turned quickly to his left. Bowman looked to his right to follow Abbott's gaze and saw the back driver's side door of the front SUV swing open and Esteban's head and shoulders appear, behind the barrel of the UMP9.

Abbott spun towards Esteban and managed to get off one shot, which missed, as he took a burst full in the chest, neck and face. A UMP9 can fire 650 nine-millimeter rounds per minute, which would empty its thirty-round magazine in less than three seconds. Bowman thought that the burst lasted about a second, which would mean about ten rounds, and most or all of them hit home. A fine red spray engulfed Abbott's head and shoulders, and he crumpled and fell, a pool of blood expanding slowly from under his still body.

"Jesus Christ!" Sanborn shouted.

Bowman felt a wave of shock, revulsion and anger pass through him, but he forced himself to maintain his composure. If he'd had a gun in his hand, he would've shot Esteban, and who knows what kind of blood bath that would've led to. Would Gordon and Sanborn have backed him up? He didn't know.

Esteban got out of the front SUV and walked back, holding his submachine gun. He prodded Abbott's body with the toe of his boot, then turned toward Gordon and unleashed a torrent of angry Spanish, waving the UMP9 in his direction. Bowman didn't know much Spanish, but he guessed that Esteban was asking why Gordon's crew hadn't killed the cop themselves. Gordon replied calmly in Spanish, and it seemed to mollify Esteban a little. After a bit more back and forth in Spanish, Esteban returned to the front SUV, which quickly pulled away.

"Jump in," Gordon said, in a strained voice. "Let's get the hell out of here." Whatever Gordon had said to Esteban had merely postponed the reckoning, and Gordon knew it.

Bowman turned to get into the SUV, and saw the branding iron in the foot well, next to the guns and his knife.

As unobtrusively as possible, while making a show of moving the guns to make room for his feet, he slid the branding iron out and dropped it on the ground next to his door, then got in and closed the door. Bowman was pretty sure that the police would find it, but he wasn't sure that they'd understand its significance, or that it would lead them to the ranch if they did. It was worth a try. Gordon was pulling away after El Chato's SUV even before Bowman got his door closed. Looking back, Bowman saw Abbott's body, a lonely mound of ruin in the middle of the road, the flashing lights of his patrol car behind him. Esteban would pay for this.

After they'd caught up with El Chato and had been driving for some time in silence Gordon, without taking his eyes from the road ahead, said, "That cop. He knew you."

It was at once a statement, a question and an accusation. Sanborn was shifting around in the back seat. Readying a weapon? Bowman resisted the urge to turn around and look, and instead turned to Gordon and spoke in a calm and unconcerned tone, or at least he hoped so.

"Yes, that was Deputy Abbott of the Bronco County Sheriff's Department. He arrested me the other day. I guess he was surprised to see me again. Can't say we struck up a friendship or anything, but I wasn't happy to see him shot down like that either."

Gordon visibly relaxed and Sanborn, taking his cue from Gordon, seemed to settle back too. They knew he'd been arrested. Abbott's recognition of Bowman meant nothing.

"It wasn't what I wanted to happen either," Gordon said, "but as far as the law is concerned, we're as guilty of killing that deputy as Esteban is."

"So now what?"

"So now we hope that El Chato forgives us for making his favorites do the dirty work this time. We're locked in now." Gordon slammed his palm against the steering wheel a few times, saying, "Damn! Damn it! God damn it!" After a minute or two of tense silence, he continued, "We have crossed the Rubicon, my friends, and there's no turning back."

"What's a Rubicon?" Sanborn asked.

CHAPTER 18

"Nothing personal, Detectives, but I've been seeing way too much of you two lately," Sheriff Cane said grimly as Carrillo and Paine ducked under the crime scene tape.

Cane had been the first on the scene. Abbott had radioed in that he'd stopped two black SUVs, given his location and asked for a report on their tag numbers. There had been no warrants outstanding for the registered owners, and the registrations appeared to match the makes and models. The dispatcher had told Cane all this, and that Abbott hadn't responded to radio calls for ten minutes. Cane told the dispatcher to call for State Police backup and headed out here in the Crown Vic as fast as he could. It still took him about twenty-five minutes. It was a big county, and most of the roads he had to take were not designed for speed.

He saw the emergency lights on Abbott's SUV and the shape in the middle of the road, and his heart sank in his chest. He wanted to vomit, and once he'd checked on Abbott, he did. It had taken the State Police another hour to get there – it was a big state – and the crime scene investigations team had taken another two. The CSI team had been working for about an hour when Carrillo and

Paine arrived, and it was nearly dusk.

"I am sorry, Sheriff," Carrillo said, as he straightened up and smoothed down his suit, which had rumpled a little as he ducked under the tape. "I did not know Deputy Abbott well, but he seemed to me to be a good man."

Paine's jacket looked a little rumpled too, but then it always did. He said nothing, but just nodded at Cane, looking sympathetic.

"He was good man," said Cane, looking down at the road between him and the two detectives and slowly shaking his head. "I knew Ken Abbott from when he was just a kid. His dad and I used to go hunting together, and sometimes Kenny would come along. Even back then he wanted to be a deputy." After a short pause, he looked up at Carrillo and added, "Maybe I shouldn't have encouraged him."

Robert Cane had been with the Bronco County Sheriff's Department for thirty years, and in all that time they'd never lost a man in the line of duty, until today. Cane's wife was with Abbott's wife, Barbara, now, but he would need to go see Barbara himself when he was done here. He owed her that. That and much more.

None of them said anything for a while, watching the CSI team at work. They'd apparently finished examining Abbott's body, for it was now in a black body bag and was being loaded into a coroner's wagon. Carrillo and Paine could clearly see the pool of vomit near where Abbott had fallen, but apparently guessed how it got there and said nothing.

Finally, Carrillo said, "We will of course get a full report from the CSI team and the State Police units that responded, Sheriff, but perhaps you could tell us what you know."

Cane took off his Stetson with one hand and ran his fingers through his hair with the other, then wiped his forehead with his shirt sleeve and replaced his hat. "When I got here, Ken's car was still running, and his emergency lights were still on. He was laying there in the middle of the road," Cane said, nodding to where Abbott's body had been, "all in a heap. I could tell right away he was dead, but I checked to be sure and then called it in. We put an APB out on the black SUVs, but so far nothing. They could've been fifty miles away by that time. The tags are both registered in the name of something called Titan Services Inc., but I'll bet dollars to donuts that'll be a shell corporation with a fake address and contact information."

Carrillo nodded. That was a common practice among drug traffickers. He dabbed lightly at his brow with a white handkerchief. He had a robin's egg blue handkerchief that matched his tie in the breast pocket of his suit jacket, but apparently that was just for show.

Paine too mopped his forehead, with a wrinkled plaid handkerchief he had pulled from one of his jacket pockets, and said, "So you think Abbott pulled over some drug traffickers by accident and found himself outnumbered and outgunned?" The handkerchief went back into a different jacket pocket, but a tail end of it protruded.

"Yep. Looks like he bit off more than he could chew. From the number and size of the shell casings, I'd say he was shot with some kind of submachine gun. Not the kind of thing your average criminal carries."

The casings had looked like nine millimeter Parabellums, like he used in his Glock, but Abbott hadn't been shot by a Glock. He'd received all of his wounds, about ten of them, in the front and while standing up, and he'd fired his gun only once. That meant some kind of automatic weapon. And in Cane's experience, an automatic weapon firing nine millimeter Parabellums meant some kind of machine pistol or submachine gun.

"El Chato's people, you think?" Paine said. The dark skin of his face was already glistening with sweat again.

"Good chance," said Cane. "I'd hate to think there was more than one gang of desperados operating in my county with this kind of firepower and a willingness to gun down a lawman."

Carrillo said, "Did you find any other physical evidence, Sheriff?"

"Well, there were some tire tracks. Maybe they'll match the casts DEA took up at the old silver mine," Cane said. "From the positions of the tire tracks and the shell casings, it looks like Abbott was alongside the rear vehicle, and he was shot from the driver's side of the front vehicle, probably from the back seat." He paused for a moment before continuing, "And there's something else, probably not connected to this at all."

"And what is that, Sheriff?"

"I found a branding iron beside the road, not too far from where Abbott was, just on the other side of where the rear vehicle was."

"For branding cattle?" Paine said. "Do they still do that?"

"They do, but this one looked like it hadn't been used in a long time. It was pretty rusty."

"So what do you make of that, Sheriff?" Carrillo asked.

"Maybe nothing. Maybe it fell off a truck some time ago and has nothing to do with this. It couldn't have been too long ago, though, because it wasn't embedded in the dirt, just sorta sitting on top of it." Cane stroked the stubble on his chin with his left hand, and then continued, "But it doesn't seem likely that the killers left it. If it was some kind of calling card they would've put it near the body, someplace more obvious. And it doesn't seem likely they'd drop it by accident, either. What kind of drug trafficker carries a branding iron around? And even if they did, how would they come to leave it here?" He pondered those questions for a few moments in silence, without arriving at any answers, then added, "But I reckon we better run it down."

"Of course, Sheriff. Did you recognize the brand?"

"No, I didn't. Looked like a rocking H, but I'm not familiar with that brand. Not many working ranches around here anymore, and none of them use that brand. But we should be able to find out who owns it. The Livestock Board keeps track of all brands in the State, so there should be a record of it."

"We will do that, Sheriff," Carrillo said, and nodded at Paine, who pulled a small notebook from an inside pocket of his jacket and jotted something down with a small stub of a pencil that seemed ill suited for Paine's big hand. The notebook and pencil went back into a different pocket of his jacket, to keep company with his handkerchief.

"Do me a favor, Detective. I know you fellas have the resources to handle this investigation, and I don't, but keep me in the loop, and let me help, if I can." Turning to go, he added, "Now I gotta go talk to Mrs. Abbott."

Cane felt sick at heart, and ten years older than he had that morning.

CHAPTER 19

José Ruíz was pacing back and forth in the kitchen of the ranch house with his hands clasped behind his back. He was waiting for Paco to return with Gordon, and thinking about how he had come to be there. Esteban was with him, standing off to the side of the room. Paco and Esteban knew his real name, and Pedro had, but very few others.

To everyone else he was El Chato, a nickname from childhood. He had forgotten why his friends had called him that, if he ever knew. It might have referred to his broad face, but that was hardly unique among the Nahua, his people. Nor were his dark bronze skin, prominent cheekbones, hooked nose and straight black hair. He was short, about five foot six inches, and stocky, again like many of his people, who had ruled the Aztec empire before the coming of the Spanish. The descendants of the Conquistadors, and of other Europeans, ruled now in Mexico, and that was, in part, why he was here.

He stopped briefly at the window that overlooked the access road and looked out, without really seeing. His mind was somewhere long ago and far away.

His parents had been campesinos, peasant farmers,

tending small patches of corn and beans. But he had always wanted more than that. He wanted wealth, power and respect. And why not? Among the Aztecs he might have been a jaguar warrior, or a great lord in a feathered cape, but modern Mexico had no place at the top for an orphaned indio like him with little education. His father had died of cholera when he was eight, and his mother had died of influenza when he was twelve. There had been distant relatives who would have taken him in, to help them work the corn and beans, but he had instead fled to the streets. The cartels always had uses for young boys, as lookouts, couriers and the like, and it paid better than any other option open to him. But more importantly, these men had wealth, power and, above all, respect.

A jackrabbit darted across the landscape outside the window, bringing his attention momentarily back to the present. He turned and started walking back across the room, his head bowed and his brows furrowed.

It had been a hard life, and he had been cruelly treated before he was strong enough to protect himself. He still burned with shame and anger when he recalled the unnatural acts that had been forced upon him by some of the older men. But he had survived and prospered. He travelled far from his village, met many people and learned much. Long before he became a man, he learned to put away childish things, to do whatever needed to be done, and to show no mercy, just as he had received none. At first, he had done what he needed to do to survive. Once he was strong enough, he had avenged the wrongs that had been done to him when he was weak. The sodomites had died slowly, and in great pain. Others had been granted a swift and painless death. He was not a monster.

Paco, Esteban and Pedro were from that early time, and had shared many of his trials. Even though they were not full-blooded indios like him, they were the only people he trusted.

Yes, he had done well, and had risen far, but he'd

reached a place from which it seemed that he could rise no further. Those above him in the cartel had connections or special talents that he could not match, and nothing that he knew how to do could be done outside the cartels, not in Mexico. And so he had come from Old Mexico to New Mexico, to make a place for himself, and Paco, Esteban and Pedro had come with him.

Lost in his thoughts, he bumped his foot into the wall at the other end of the room and pulled up short, startled. He quickly looked over at Esteban, to see if he had noticed, but Esteban was intently studying his fingernails. If he had seen El Chato's embarrassing stumble, he was pretending he hadn't. El Chato walked to the wooden table in the middle of the room and sat down at a chair facing the door. Paco seemed to be taking a long time to fetch Gordon.

He had been to America many times, to sell drugs to the gringos, and had made many connections. The cartel found it easier to deal with him than with the Americans, so he had positioned himself as a middleman, buying from the cartel in large batches and selling to the gringos in smaller batches. It was a profitable business, and there were many advantages to operating in America. He was no longer under the direction or control of the cartels, although they could certainly reach out and swat him if they chose to, and he did not have the risk and expense of smuggling the drugs across the border.

But there were disadvantages as well. In Mexico, the police were much more manageable. Most of them were either on the payroll of the cartel or too afraid to interfere with the cartel's business. It was necessary from time to time to reinforce that fear, by punishing those who caused trouble, and the most effective punishment was to kill a man's family. Even the bravest man, who does not fear for his own life, could be made to fear for the life of his wife, his mother, or his child.

He had tried bribery, with some limited success. But it

was not easy, because of the cultural differences and the small size of his organization. It was difficult to approach the right persons, and those persons were less willing than in Mexico to accept bribes. That would change with time, he thought, once the authorities realized that his organization and others like it were here to stay. And when that pendejo Walker of the DEA had caused the loss of so much merchandise and the arrest of some of his business partners, he had tried fear, by having his wife and daughter killed. El Chato wondered now if that had been a mistake. He had been angry, and had not thought it through properly. The immediate consequence of those killings would be increased efforts by the law, and more trouble for him. To create a climate of fear that would protect his organization from interference, he needed to show that he could do the same to others at will, and he did not have the resources to do that. Not yet. Perhaps if he had a dozen men like Hawk, he could do it, but he did not think there were a dozen men like Hawk, men who enjoyed hurting and killing.

He considered whether to receive Gordon standing or sitting. Which would best convey his authority? Sitting, surely, while Gordon was forced to stand. He got up from his seat, walked around the table and moved the two chairs on the other side to the ends of the table, then went back to his seat facing the door.

He had been angry when he killed Walker, and that also had been a mistake. Walker had killed Pedro, had cut his throat like he was butchering a pig. El Chato had taken his revenge for that, but he should have questioned him first. He suspected that someone in his organization, or perhaps in the organization of one of his business partners, was providing information to the DEA. How else could they have known enough to launch the raid that had cost him so much money and trouble? But who in his organization could be working with the DEA? He trusted his Mexican inner circle completely, and in any case they were always with him. Of the gringos, only Hawk had the opportunity, since he was occasionally off by himself on errands that required his special aptitudes. But El Chato could not imagine Hawk working with the law; he was guilty of too much that the law would find unforgivable. No, it could not be any of his people; it must be someone working for one of his business partners. Walker had been in a position to know, and he would have told El Chato what he knew. Walker had been a brave man, he had to admit, but everyone talks eventually, with the proper persuasion. It was too late for that now, though, and all because of his anger.

The need for someone like Gordon was another disadvantage of operating in America. In Mexico, it had been easy to recruit for his organization. There were always those eager for the chance, men like the young man he had been, and it was easy to find them. In America it was not so easy. He was isolated from the culture, even the Hispanic culture. Mexicans who had come to America, whether legally or not, kept their distance from his people. The kind that he was looking for, men who were not willing to work like a campesino for a pittance, had not left Mexico. So he needed someone like Gordon, to recruit men for him, men who were familiar with weapons and knew how to provide security. And Gordon had done well in the eight months or so he had worked for him. He had recruited all of the other Americans, and managed them. They looked professional, which was all that was needed most of the time, and he did not doubt that they would perform well if a transaction turned bad. They had proved themselves when Walker had attacked. But today was the first time that they had directly encountered the law. Walker did not count, as they didn't know that he was a DEA agent. Today, Gordon had failed him, and it had been left to Esteban to do what needed to be done.

If this had happened in Mexico, he would have killed Gordon, as an example for the others. But he did not know how the other Americans would react to that, and he still needed Gordon to manage them and recruit others. Hawk was reliable, he thought, but the others did not seem to like or trust him. He was not a leader of men. If all of the Americans decided at once to turn on him, they could kill him, along with Paco and Esteban. He could kill them all instead, of course, if he acted first, but then he would have to start over. No, he did not want to kill Gordon, at least not yet. If Gordon showed the right attitude, he would try to improve him, and keep a close eye on all of the gringos, with Hawk's help.

Gordon himself came into the room then, followed by Paco. Paco moved off to the left, so that he and Esteban were on either side of and a little behind Gordon. His expression was grim, but if he was afraid he was doing a good job of hiding it. Gordon still had his pistol on him, and El Chato considered whether he should have Gordon disarmed, but thought better of it. It would be a sign of weakness and fear. If Gordon chose to kill him, he could probably do so, but would immediately be cut down by Paco and Esteban.

Gordon said nothing, waiting for El Chato to begin. El Chato spoke some English, but Paco and Esteban spoke little and Gordon's Spanish was better than El Chato's English, so he spoke in Spanish now.

"You disappointed me today, Señor Gordon."

"I am sorry to hear you say so, Jefe. In what way have I disappointed you?"

"You allowed a Deputy Sheriff to interfere with our business. Only Esteban's actions corrected the problem."

"And what would you have had me do?"

"I would have had you do what Esteban did," El Chato said testily, "and not leave it to others to do your job."

"Killing policemen is not what I signed up for, Jefe."

"You signed up to protect me and my people!" El Chato shouted, rising from his chair. "And that policeman was a threat!" Gordon stiffened, but didn't otherwise move. Paco and Esteban shuffled their feet in the ensuing silence.

After a few moments, Gordon said, sounding chastened, "I had not considered what I should do in that situation. I was not prepared for it."

El Chato stared at Gordon for several seconds, his black eyes burning with rage and the muscles in his face twitching, as he tried to gain control of his temper.

Finally, El Chato's face relaxed and he sat back down. In a calmer voice, he said, "Very well, I accept that. But you must make a decision now, Señor Gordon. You must commit to providing security, against any and all threats, or you must resign from my service." After a moment, he continued, "So what is your decision, Señor Gordon?"

Without hesitation, Gordon said, "In the future, I will do all that is necessary, Jefe."

El Chato nodded. He did not know whether Gordon was sincere. Surely he knew what El Chato had meant by "resign." El Chato could not allow someone who knew as much about his operation as Gordon did simply to leave. Gordon had said what he had to say to survive another day. But that was enough for now. He had gotten the message.

"Then we will say no more about the matter. Tell me about this new man that you have found, the one who calls himself Archer. He did not approach you?"

Gordon seemed to relax a bit. He must have realized that he had survived this episode. "No, we approached him, like all the others," Gordon said. That was a basic precaution. A man that came looking for a job might be working for a competitor, or the law. "And he refused at first. I do not think he would have done that if he were some kind of plant."

"And yet," El Chato said, "he met with the police after he refused and before he changed his mind. Is that not suspicious?"

"He did not meet with the police. He was arrested."

"And then released," said El Chato. "Perhaps they came to some arrangement. Perhaps they said 'bring us El Chato and we will not charge you with this crime,' or offered him some kind of reward." He looked inquiringly at Gordon, his eyebrows raised and his head tilted a little to the side.

"It is possible," said Gordon, "but I do not think the police operate like that." Perhaps not in America, thought El Chato. "I searched him, of course, and did not find any wires or anything like that."

El Chato knew that Archer could not be the one who had been providing the DEA with information, since he had only just arrived, but he could be a DEA plant nonetheless. He had not had many opportunities to observe Archer yet, but he seemed different than the other gringos Gordon had recruited, more observant and thoughtful. He could be a dangerous enemy, or a valuable asset.

"I am sure you are correct, Señor Gordon," El Chato said, and made a mental note to have Hawk search Archer's belongings again, "but let us keep an eye on this Archer, just in case. Do not give him any opportunities to communicate with anyone outside our little group, until we are more sure of him."

"Sí, jefe." Gordon nodded.

"That will be all, Señor Gordon," El Chato said, with a backward wave of his hand. "Please ask Señor Hawk to come to see me."

Gordon nodded again and left the ranch house. After he had left, El Chato spoke to Paco and Esteban.

"What do you think of Señor Gordon, my friends? Do you think he will behave appropriately in the future?"

"I do not trust him, Chato," said Esteban. "I do not trust any of the gringos, not even Hawk."

Paco nodded his agreement, frowning.

"I do not trust them either, my friends, and so we must be constantly on our guard. Any sign of betrayal or disloyalty must be dealt with immediately and severely," El Chato said, and drew his hand across his throat in a cutting motion to emphasize his point.

There was a knock on the door, and Paco opened it. It was Hawk, and Paco motioned for him to come in.

"You looking for me, boss?" Hawk said. He had a smug, self-satisfied look. There was none of the tension so evident in Gordon a few moments earlier.

Hawk knew no Spanish, so El Chato replied in heavily accented English. "Yes, mister Hawk. I have for you a little job. This mister Archer, who recently join us, you no like him, I think."

"You got that right, boss. You want me to kill him?" His smug grin broadened and he briefly touched the handle of his tomahawk, which hung down under his left arm.

El Chato noticed the gesture, and frowned. Hawk was useful, but he was more of butcher than a surgeon, and would have to be restrained.

"No, mister Hawk, not if only for your pride. But perhaps – if there is another reason. I fear maybe he is working for the police. I want you to look at his things that he brought with him. Maybe he has a wire or something. Wait till no one can see you, and tell me if you find something. If he is with the police, I will let you kill him."

"Will do, boss, and here's hoping."

CHAPTER 20

Bowman unscrewed the gas cap from the generator and set it aside, then unscrewed the cap from the five-gallon gas can and picked it up. It was the morning after the killing of Abbott, and Gordon had asked him to top up the generator, which was in a separate room in the barn. It occupied the left front quadrant, and was about twenty feet square. The generator was in the front left corner of the room, and the exhaust was vented out through a small hole in the wall.

Bowman heard the door close and latch, and turned quickly to see Hawk pointing a pistol at him and leering triumphantly. In his left hand, Hawk held something small and thin between his thumb and forefinger, but Bowman couldn't make out what it was in the dim light. Hawk's tomahawk was slung under his left arm. Bowman had his Beretta and knife, but neither was in his hand. Hawk must have followed him here, to take his revenge. He'd been careless, letting Hawk get the drop on him with no one else around. This would be a pathetic way to die.

The door, which Hawk had just closed and latched, was in the corner opposite the generator. There was one dirty window on the outside wall, which let in some of the morning light, and a single bare bulb, currently unlit, hung from a cord slung over a large nail driven into a ceiling joist in the center of the room. Apart from the generator, there were some shelves and tables along the walls containing various supplies, turpentine, old paint and ropes, and several old pieces of equipment of one kind or another. But mostly the room was empty, and nothing stood between Hawk in his corner and Bowman in his.

"Put the gas can down and step away from the generator, asshole. I don't want to start a fire."

Bowman did neither. He wasn't going to cooperate in his own murder. But he had to do something. All he could think to do was to keep Hawk talking, to buy some time while considered his options.

"You still mad about that beating I administered? I would think a surly little prick like you would be used to that by now." Bowman didn't expect this response to improve Hawk's attitude, but it did help Bowman maintain his own composure. He knew that Hawk could easily kill him, and very much wanted to, but he didn't want Hawk to think he was cowed. He didn't want to die, but if he had to die it would not be while begging for his life. "And the boss is not going to like you killing a valued member of the crew just to soothe your injured pride." That, Bowman thought, was his best argument under the circumstances. He probably should've led with it, but Hawk wasn't the only one in the room with some pride.

Hawk's eyes flashed with anger for a moment, but he quickly reverted to his initial look of smug satisfaction. He held up his left hand and showed the card he was holding. Bowman couldn't see it clearly, but realized that it must be the card that DEA Special Agent Bates had given him. He'd forgotten that he had it. Hawk must have searched his bag and found it in the clothes he was wearing when Bates had given him her card. Those clothes hadn't been in his bag when Gordon had searched it, and Gordon had missed it when he patted him down before blindfolding him.

"The boss is going to thank me for killing a DEA plant, Archer. Resolving our personal quarrel is just a little bonus for me."

Bowman's mind raced. The truth was that he wasn't a DEA plant, not really, and the card proved no such thing. Hawk had stumbled onto something close to the truth, but for the wrong reasons. If this wasn't just about revenge, he might be able to talk his way out of it. He wouldn't beg, but he would try to reason with him.

"I see you found that DEA agent's card. Congratulations. What is that supposed to prove? You knew I was arrested and questioned about the murders. I told her what I knew, which was nothing, and then she gave me her card and said to call her if I had anything to add. I forgot I had it, or I would have tossed it by now. You think the DEA sends someone to infiltrate a gang and has them carry a DEA agent's card with them?" Bowman wanted to add something like 'dumbass,' but decided that he'd antagonized Hawk enough for now.

Hawk's face fell, and he glared at Bowman. He may be an ass, but he's not dumb, Bowman thought; he must have realized that what Bowman said was true. Bowman began to hope that he might live another day. After a few moments, however, the gloom on Hawk's face lifted and the familiar leer reappeared.

"It really doesn't matter, though, does it?" he said. "You'll be dead. I'll say I confronted you with this card and you attacked me. So I killed you." He paused, enjoying himself, and then continued, "But I'm not going to shoot you," he said, as he put the card in his shirt pocket and then touched his tomahawk with his left hand, "I'm going to kill you with this, and I'm going to enjoy it."

Bowman knew that any chance of talking his way out of this had disappeared, or rather that there never had been a chance. There was no longer any reason to avoid antagonizing Hawk. Provoking his anger might actually help, if it caused him to act rashly. In any case, the longer they spent trading insults the longer he would be alive, and while there is life there is hope.

"I bet you would enjoy it, you sick bastard, just like you enjoyed killing that woman and the little girl."

It was a guess, but Bowman thought it was a good guess, and it was rewarded by a fleeting look of surprise on Hawk's face, quickly replaced by his smug leer. But it was enough. Bowman was certain that he was right, and that gave this encounter a whole new meaning. This was why he was here, he realized, to find and confront the killer. He could not undo what he'd done in Iraq, but this he could do, and he felt a great weight lift from him, a weight that he hadn't realized was there until then. Even if he were killed here and now, at least his death would have some larger meaning.

"So you are here on some kind of mission after all," Hawk said. "All the more reason to kill you." The leer faded away, to leave dead, snake-like eyes and a straight, hard mouth. "Now put down the gas can and take off your belt. And no sudden moves."

Bowman bent to set the gas can and gas cap down on the floor, then straightened up. He thought of trying to go for his gun, maybe diving to the side as he reached for it. It wasn't likely to work, but it would be better than being shot down without putting up a fight. But Hawk had said that he wouldn't shoot him, and Bowman thought that he would've shot him by now if he were going to. Facing the tomahawk seemed like his best chance, especially if he had his knife.

"Tomahawk versus knife?" he said. "Or do you prefer your victims to be defenseless?"

This brought some life to Hawk's eyes, which sparkled with eager anticipation.

"By all means, Archer, keep your knife, but take off your gun before I change my mind and just shoot you."

Bowman unbuckled his belt and pulled it through his

belt loops and the loops holding his gun and knife, which fell to the floor. Then he dropped his belt.

"Now kick your gun over to me."

Bowman kicked his gun and holster over towards Hawk's feet, and Hawk kicked it behind him, towards the door.

"What about your own gun?" Bowman asked. "Going to hang onto it in case you change your mind? Killing me with your little hatchet may not be as easy as you think."

Hawk glared at him, and for a moment Bowman thought Hawk was going to shoot him after all. Had he overplayed his hand, and pushed Hawk too hard? He was walking a fine line that he couldn't see, and could barely sense.

But after a few moments Hawk's leer returned, and he tossed his own gun behind him and pulled his tomahawk from its sheath under his left arm. Whatever else Hawk might be, he wasn't a coward.

Bowman realized that he had been holding his breath, and took a moment to steady himself. Then he stooped and picked up his knife. As he straightened up, he drew it from its sheath, which he tossed aside. Things were looking up. The odds were still against him, but he now had a fighting chance. With his free left hand, he touched the little gold Jesus at his neck, and then stepped away from the generator. He didn't want to be forced into a corner, where Hawk could pin him down and slash at him with the long-handled tomahawk. He needed to get in close, where the longer reach of the tomahawk would not be an advantage, and swinging it would be difficult. In close, he could stab with his knife while the tomahawk would be almost useless. But to get there, he needed to pass through the killing zone, where the tomahawk's extra reach and power could kill or disable him before he was close enough to use his knife. In the meantime, he needed room to maneuver to avoid that brutal heavy blade on the front of the axe head and the spear point on the back.

Hawk moved forward quickly in a low crouch, swinging his weapon from side to side, forcing Bowman to jump back, trying to corner him. He was getting closer with every swing, until a sharp pain in Bowman's left side, just above the lowest rib, informed him that Hawk had finally drawn blood. Bowman tried to thrust at Hawk after the cutting swing had passed, but Hawk's back swing was quick and vicious, and caught the edge of his right shoulder, drawing more blood.

Hawk smiled as he saw the blood, and his eyes gleamed.

Bowman was running out of room, and knew that he would be running out of blood as well if this continued. He was tempted to rush Hawk, and end it one way or the other, but he had to resist. Time was on his side. With time, perhaps he could think of a plan, or some help would arrive.

Bowman saw a work table on his left, to the right of the generator, and above the table was the sole window. He leapt up onto the table and kicked back with his heel to shatter the glass. Hawk could be on him with his tomahawk before he could pull himself through the window, he knew, but maybe kicking out the pane would raise an alarm and bring some help. There were some old coffee cans filled with nuts and bolts on the table, and he kicked them at Hawk, who dodged and stepped back a pace. Bowman used the space to jump down from the table to his left and quickly turned to face Hawk again. He'd escaped from the corner he'd started in, but the process began again, with Hawk scything back and forth with his tomahawk and Bowman jumping back or to the side to avoid the heavy blade.

He would've traded his knife for that branding iron, or something like it that he could use as a club, or a mace. Even better would be something that he could use as a shield. That would allow him to get in close and use his knife. But he saw nothing that would serve either purpose.

Occasionally he was able to snatch up one of the bolts he'd scattered and throw it at Hawk. It helped to keep him back, but not much, and not for long. It must have looked pretty pathetic, and it seemed to amuse Hawk, rather than annoy him. So far, Bowman had managed to stay out of the back corner, but he was being forced up against the back wall. To his left was the door and, about ten feet away, the two pistols.

"Your fancy knife isn't doing you much good, is it, Archer? And your ridiculous hopping around is just extending the fun." Hawk was clearly confident, and was enjoying himself.

Bowman wasn't confident, and he wasn't enjoying this. But he was focused and in the moment, and there was no room for fear. This had always been his experience with combat. Once the battle was joined, the fear and dread would lift, and be replaced by an intense focus on the here and now.

And now he was focusing on the pistols. He thought that he could reach one of them in one lunge from where he stood, but knew that Hawk could follow and bury the tomahawk in his back or head before he could bring the pistol to bear. Hawk seemed to know what Bowman was thinking. He was blocking Bowman from getting any nearer to the pistols, but not cutting him off entirely. He seemed to want Bowman to make the attempt.

And Bowman did.

He lunged towards the nearer pistol, his holstered Beretta. He didn't try to grab it, but instead aimed for a spot a little past the gun and rolled quickly to the side as he landed. He was counting on Hawk to leap for the spot where the gun was, and he did, bringing the tomahawk blade down on the floor boards where Bowman's chest or head would've been if he'd wasted a moment attempting to retrieve the gun. Bowman was already rolling back as Hawk realized his mistake and tried to scramble away to create some distance for his tomahawk.

But it was too late. Bowman was on him and the two of them were rolling on the floor, locked in a desperate embrace. Bowman had his left arm over Hawk's right shoulder and across his back, and his head on the other side of Hawk's head, ear to ear, holding him in a tight bear hug. Bowman stabbed again and again as Hawk vainly tried to fend off the knife with his left hand and counterattack with the tomahawk in his right. The only sounds were their wordless grunts of effort and of pain.

Bowman felt his knife slide into the soft flesh below Hawk's ribs, and he pulled it out and raised it higher for the next thrust. His blade struck the ribs, and he twisted it as he pushed, until it slid in between two ribs, and then he worked it back and forth before pulling it out for another thrust. Hawk managed to drag the tomahawk blade across Bowman's back and legs, but didn't have the room to put any power into it.

Soon, and abruptly, Hawk seemed to deflate and his struggles ceased. Bowman rolled off of him, exhausted and shaking.

The battle was over, and all the fear and revulsion that had been held at bay came flooding in, mixed now with relief and elation.

Even as his mind was still getting around this new situation, the door burst open and Gordon rushed in, followed immediately by El Chato, Paco and Esteban. They saw Hawk splayed out on his back, still holding his bloody tomahawk, his dead eyes staring at the ceiling. His torso was drenched in bright red blood, which dripped onto the floorboards on either side of his body. Bowman lay just on the other side of him. Like Hawk, he was still holding his knife and he and it were covered in blood. But unlike Hawk, his eyes were very much alive, and he was gasping for breath. El Chato drew his pistol and waved it around excitedly, shouting angrily in Spanish.

After quickly taking in the scene, Gordon exclaimed, "What the hell happened here!?"

171

With an effort, Bowman pulled himself up to a sitting position and gasped, "He jumped me – like he'd been wanting to do – since I busted his face." Then, as quickly as he could while still gasping for breath, he told Gordon what had happened, other than the part about the DEA agent's card and Hawk's accusation. It seemed wisest to leave that part out for the time being. Gordon translated this for El Chato. The explanation didn't seem to make him any less angry, however, and he continued to shout and gesticulate with the pistol.

"He's not happy, Archer," Gordon said to Bowman, after some back and forth with El Chato. "Hawk was his favorite among us Americans, and he's not so sure about you. He may kill you for this, if he doesn't calm down soon." With his eyes, Gordon seemed to add 'and I can't help you.'

Bowman could see from the way El Chato was acting that Gordon was right. He was stomping around in a small circle, yelling angrily and periodically pointing his gun at Bowman or talking to Paco, who was kneeling by Hawk's body and examining his wounds. Finally, he seemed to make up his mind, and pointed his gun at Bowman's head.

Hawk was dead, but El Chato was the man that had ordered the killings, and who had tried to kill Walker. Bowman had made a good start by killing Hawk. He'd won this battle, but not the war, and it looked like the war might be over for him. Bowman knew that nothing he could say to El Chato would make any difference, even if he could speak Spanish, and he would not plead for his life. But if El Chato was going to kill him, he was going to have to look him in the eye as he did so.

So Bowman looked up at El Chato, past the barrel of the gun pointed at his head. It wasn't a pleading look, for he was too proud for that, nor a fearful look, for he wasn't afraid. It wasn't even an angry look, for he was too tired for that. It was a reproachful look, and it seemed to surprise El Chato. His trigger finger relaxed for an instant, and in that instant Paco spoke.

"Momento, Jefe," he said and showed El Chato a bloody card that he'd just fished from Hawk's breast pocket. It was the card that Agent Bates had given Bowman.

Paco and El Chato were examining the card and looking down at Hawk's body, talking excitedly. Bowman couldn't understand much of what they said, but it was clear that they were surprised and angry. He gradually realized that they were angry at Hawk now, not him. El Chato started kicking Hawk's body and cursing. After a few minutes of this, he growled some instructions to Gordon and stormed out, followed by Paco and Esteban.

Bowman watched them go. He was tired and confused, and he felt like the air had been let out of him.

"What the hell just happened?" he asked Gordon, when the two of them were alone.

"You almost got your head perforated," Gordon said, "and then they found a card on Hawk with some contact info for a DEA agent. Looks like the little prick was working both sides of the fence. I'd never have guessed. He didn't seem like the type to work with the law."

"No, he didn't," Bowman said.

"Looks like Chato's beef with you for killing Hawk sort of melted away once it turned out that Hawk wasn't the golden boy he thought he was. He told me to have somebody bury what's left of him out in the desert. I don't think there will be many mourners at the funeral. But let's get you cleaned up first; you look like you got caught in a blood storm. Are you hurt, or is that all Hawk's blood?"

"Most of it, but I could use a few stitches here and there."

"My specialty," Gordon said, and helped Bowman to his feet.

No, the war is not over, Bowman thought, as he stiffly

and painfully followed Gordon out of the generator room, but I've made some good progress and lived to fight another day.

CHAPTER 21

"That is Detective Carrillo on the line, Sheriff," Mrs. Flores said, "Can you take the call?"

"Yes, thank you, Rosa," Cane said, and picked up the phone on his desk. "Good afternoon, Detective, what can I do for you?"

"I have some news for you, Sheriff, and a request."

"I'll help any way I can, but let's start with the news. Good news, I hope."

"Interesting news. We were able to pull some finger prints from that branding iron you found at the scene of Deputy Abbott's murder, and we found a match. You took those prints just the other day, Sheriff. They belong to one Robert Roy Bowman, most recently of Page, Montana, current location unknown." Carrillo paused to let Cane absorb that information, and then continued, "So what do you make of that, Sheriff?"

This was interesting news, but was it good news or bad? Cane sat back in his chair and thought through the possibilities. It was still just possible that the branding iron had nothing to do with Abbott's murder, but the odds of that now seemed vanishingly small. And that possibility wasn't worth pursuing, because it led nowhere, so he assumed that it was related to the murder. That meant that Bowman was there, with the branding iron, when Abbott was murdered. But why was Bowman there? Was he working for El Chato after all? Had he fooled them all? Cane didn't think so. He thought he was a good judge of character, and his gut told him that Bowman would not sign up with an outfit like that. And that idea didn't fit with Bowman's efforts to save Walker. So then why was he there? Had they kidnapped him? He rubbed his scalp with his free hand, as if to stimulate his brain cells, and closed his eyes tight as he focused on the problem.

And then Cane remembered Bowman's suggestion to Agent Clementine Bates, the suggestion that she had immediately rejected. So Bowman had infiltrated El Chato's organization and had left the branding iron at the scene, whether by accident or on purpose. He could've accidentally dropped it, but why would he have it with him in the first place, and how do you drop a branding iron without noticing? If he left it at the scene on purpose, it would explain why he had it, to use it as a signal of some kind. A brand was unique to a ranch, so Bowman was pointing them to a particular ranch.

"Sheriff?"

Cane opened his eyes and sat up in his chair. "I'm still here, just been noodling this little puzzle." After a short pause he continued, "I think, Detective, that our boy is playing secret agent, and is trying to lead us to the bad guys."

"I think so too, Sheriff. And so we must find the ranch associated with that brand, and as quickly as possible. If we are right, Mr. Bowman is playing a dangerous game and will need our help. He seemed like a competent young man, but he is swimming in turbulent waters."

"So what have you learned about the brand? A rocking H, if I don't miss my guess."

"Yes, Sheriff, a rocking H. That brand was indeed registered with the Livestock Board, as you suggested. It was registered in the name of a Mr. Caleb Lewis. Mr. Lewis died some twenty years ago, and the registration had not been renewed since some ten years prior to that. The only address on record was a post office box in Tierra Roja. The postmaster confirmed that a Caleb Lewis had maintained that post office box for many years, but had no further information. So far, we have not been able to identify any living relations of Mr. Lewis. We will continue our investigation, Sheriff, but for the moment we are at an impasse, which brings me to my request."

"Just ask and you shall receive. This case is priority one with me until we catch them murdering sonsabitches."

"Thank you, Sheriff. It seems to me that we need to talk to someone who is familiar with the ranches and ranchers in Bronco County that were active thirty or forty years ago. I thought you would be best situated to follow that line of inquiry."

"Of course. I think I know just the man. I'll go see him now and let you know as soon as I've learned anything."

As soon as they'd hung up, Cane picked up his hat and headed out the door. As he passed Mrs. Flores, he said, "Rosa, I'll be up at my dad's place."

Cane would be driving, because his father had no phone. He didn't have any electricity or running water, either. He hadn't always lived like that. When Robert Cane was growing up, they lived like everyone else, with all the modern conveniences. But when his mother had died some ten years ago, his father had moved into what had been his hunting camp, and rarely ventured out. For a while, Sheriff Cane had tried to convince him to move into town, to be closer to him and others that could help him. He was too old to be living like that. But he'd finally given up, because that was what his father wanted, and he was a grown man. Sheriff Cane thought that maybe living like that reminded him of his youth, or maybe he just found it more peaceful. He lived a solitary life now, but when he was younger he seemed to know everybody, and to never forget a name or a face. If anyone could tell him where Caleb Lewis' ranch was, it was Earnest Cane.

It took him about twenty minutes to get there, the last few hundred yards over a winding dirt track that led nowhere else. He flushed a grouse on the way in, and it startled him a little as it burst out of its ground cover right in front of his vehicle. Grouse and quail were what they'd hunted mostly, back when they hunted. Big game, like deer, sheep and elk, mostly kept to the higher country. Now the hunting camp was just a place to live.

As Cane pulled up to the cabin in the Sheriff's Department SUV he saw his father standing on the porch, cradling a double-barreled shotgun in his arms. He was wearing what he always wore these days, a pair of overalls over a light blue shirt. He must have just stepped out onto the porch, because he was hatless and wore a pair of leather slippers. His hair was white, but he had a full head of it still, which he kept neatly trimmed, and his face was clean shaven. Dad prides himself on keeping himself neat, thought Cane, even though there's no one to notice most of the time.

"Expecting trouble, Dad?" Cane said, as he climbed out of the SUV.

"Wasn't expecting company, Bobby." His father and a few uncles and aunts were the only ones that still called him Bobby. Some old friends called him Bob, but he preferred Robert, and that's how he introduced himself these days. "You were here just a couple of days ago, and I don't get many other visitors."

That was true, thought Cane, and he inwardly winced with guilt. His father had outlived most friends and family of his generation. Cane visited him at least once a week, and brought supplies as needed, but he should really make an effort to come more often. He'd tried to convince his father to come live with him and his wife, but with no success. The old man was in his mid-eighties now, and there might not be many more opportunities to spend time with him.

"Official business this time, Dad. Got any coffee on?"

"Come on in and I'll put some on," his father said, and they walked into the cabin together. His father returned the shotgun to the gun rack and walked slowly over to the corner of the cabin that served as the kitchen. Cane knew better than to offer to help. His father was slower than he had been, but he could still take care of himself and was proud of the fact. As his father put the coffee pot on the small propane camp stove Cane looked around the cabin, which consisted of a single room and a sleeping loft. Cane and his father had slept up in that loft many times over the years, but his father didn't use it now. A few years ago, Cane had brought one of the beds down to the lower level for him. His father had made a show of claiming that it wasn't necessary, that he could get up and down from the loft just fine, but he'd acquiesced and no longer attempted the stairs. Apart from the bed, the cabin, like most hunting cabins, was furnished with castaway furniture and odds and ends. But the bed was neatly made and the place looked clean and tidy. Cane told himself that he would insist that his father come live with him as soon as he detected any sign that his father couldn't, or wouldn't, take care of himself properly. There was no sign of that yet.

Cane took a seat at the kitchen table and said, "You remember Ken Abbott?"

"Willie's boy? Of course I remember him, he's been up here hunting with us more than once. One of your deputies now, right?"

"Yeah, Dad. He was killed yesterday, in the line of duty." Had he really said that? thought Cane, 'killed in the line of duty?' It seemed too formal, too cold.

"Oh God, I'm sorry, Bobby," his father said, turning from the stove to look at Cane. "What happened?"

"We think he pulled over some drug traffickers. Whoever it was shot him, with a submachine gun, I think.

He never had a chance."

His father walked over to the table with two mismatched, slightly chipped coffee mugs. As he put them on the table, Cane could see his father's hands quiver a little, just perceptibly. Then he sat down and put one atop the other on the table, to settle them down. "The coffee will be another couple of minutes." After a short pause, he continued, "I guess it's a blessing of sorts that Willie and Jan aren't alive to see this. No parents should have to bury their child. How's Ken's wife holding up?"

"As well as can be expected, I guess. The ladies are tag teaming her to make sure she always has company. It'll take some time, but I reckon she'll be OK."

"It's a hell of a thing."

"Sure is, Dad. Ken is the first and only deputy I've ever lost. It's a hell of a thing, indeed."

The coffee began to percolate, and they both listened in silence for a few moments.

"So it sounds like you haven't caught the killers yet."

"Not yet, Dad. That's why I'm here. I need your help."

"I can't imagine how I could help, but I will if I can. What do you need?"

"I need information, Dad, something you would know if anyone would." His father nodded, and Cane continued, "We found a branding iron at the scene, an iron for the Rocking H brand. We think that if we can locate the ranch that used that brand we can locate the killers."

Cane was about to tell his father the name in which the brand was registered, but his father beat him to it. "Why, that would be Caleb Lewis' brand. I may have used that iron myself. I used to work on the Lewis ranch from time to time during the war, when most of the regular hands were overseas. I was just a teenager, too young to sign up for the war but old enough to ride and rope and wrangle." He paused for a few moments, looking into his empty coffee mug and apparently casting his mind back over the years. "At the time, I was foolish enough to be jealous of them cowboys, the ones that went off to the war. A lot of them didn't come back, and some that did left some parts of themselves behind." After another pause, he continued, "But I got my share in Korea, I guess."

"You sure did, Dad." That had been before Cane was born, and his father hadn't talked about it much, but Cane had heard enough to know that his father had indeed gotten his share in Korea. He'd been at Chosin Reservoir with the First Marine Division. One of the 'Chosin Few.' Encircled by a Red Chinese army four times their number, they'd fought their way out in seventeen days of brutal combat in temperatures as low as thirty-five degrees below zero. He'd gotten more than his share.

Cane noticed that the coffee had stopped percolating. He stood up, walked over to turn off the stove and get the coffee pot, and came back and filled their mugs. The trick to helping his father without bruising his feelings, Cane had learned, was to not ask, but to just do it.

"But that ranch went under a long time ago, like most of the ranches around here, and Caleb's been dead almost as long. Don't think he left any family, either. Not sure what became of the ranch. I know it's not a working ranch anymore."

Cane put the coffee pot back on the stove and came back and sat down across from his father.

"We think the killers may be holed up at that ranch, Dad. Do you remember where it was?"

"Of course I do, and I can draw you a map of what it looked like last time I saw it."

The man is still sharp as a tack, Cane thought as he watched his father draw the map and listened to him describe what he remembered of the Rocking H Ranch. There were still real cowboys in those days, though it was already well past the glory days of the Wild West. Through his father, Cane felt a connection to that time that he'd never felt before. It somehow seemed more real to him now, and he liked that. His father had led an interesting life, and was full of great stories. He must try to tease some more out of him soon, while he had the chance.

Those hands could tell a story all their own. They shook a little now, as he worked on the map, but they were still the hands that Cane remembered growing up: big, thickly veined, calloused, strong and reassuring. They were tools, never weapons. His father did not hug, but one of those hands on your shoulder could convey just as much.

Finally, and sooner than he wanted to, Cane stood up and said, "Well, Dad, I best be going. I got a lot to arrange before it gets too late."

His father stood up as well and walked him to the door. As Cane put his hat on and was about to step outside, the old man put a hand on his shoulder and said, "You be careful, Bobby."

"Always, Dad. Always."

As he drove back to town, Cane thought about what he needed to do. It would be dark soon, and it was too late to go out to the ranch today. He needed to coordinate with the State Police and DEA and plan for a visit to the ranch first thing in the morning. In the meantime, he would post a deputy to watch the access road, to make sure no one left that ranch before he got there. It would be a big production, and he would look like a fool if all they found was an abandoned ranch. But he could live with that.

CHAPTER 22

Bowman winced as Gordon tightened a stitch. "Stop being such a little girl," Gordon said. "I can see these aren't the first stitches you've gotten."

"No, but usually I get some local anesthetic."

"You want me to find you a stick to bite on?" Bowman shook his head, and Gordon continued, "Then quit your whining. All your wounds are slash wounds, no puncture wounds, and none of them deep. You should live."

They were sitting on a couple of chairs at a little table in the bunkhouse. The other Americans were on sentry duty, and the Mexicans were in the ranch house, so they had the bunkhouse to themselves. Gordon had gotten a pail of water from the well and had helped Bowman clean off the blood. Most of it was Hawk's, but plenty of it was Bowman's. His shirt and pants were a total loss, and he sat in his boxer shorts as Gordon stitched and bandaged his wounds. Some of them could be closed with butterfly bandages, but a few required stitches.

"We don't get many religious types in this outfit," said Gordon, glancing at the little gold Jesus around Bowman's neck.

"It belonged to a friend of mine. It's kind of a memento."

"I understand."

Bowman could tell that he did understand, as only someone who had been in a similar situation could understand.

"You ever do this before?" Bowman asked. "Stitch up wounds, I mean."

"A few times. My own, once or twice. Sometimes we'd be out for days, and couldn't go home early just to get a few stitches. These scars may be uglier than they needed to be, but you won't leak too much."

"Special Forces? You get your Yarborough knife for free?"

"Sit up straight. The skin on your back is too tight for this."

Bowman, who had been leaning over the card table, on his elbows, sat up straight. He and grimaced as Gordon started another stitch.

"Yeah. But I don't think I'd call it free." Gordon said. "How about yourself? Army or Marines? I don't see any anchor tattoos, so I'm guessing Army."

"Yes, Army," Bowman said. He wanted to learn more about Gordon, and didn't want to talk about himself, so he didn't give any particulars, and instead said, "So how did you come to speak Spanish so well? You don't look Mexican."

"Not all Mexicans look like those three," Gordon said, nodding in the direction of the ranch house. "But no, I'm not Mexican. I'm Cuban, or my family is. I was born in Miami, but my parents came from Cuba, and we spoke Spanish at home."

"Are they still in Miami?"

"Yes," Gordon said, and then lapsed into silence as he continued to work on Bowman's wounds. After a while, he said, "So what are you doing here, my friend?"

Bowman stiffened, but Gordon continued calmly to

work on Bowman's wounds as if he hadn't noticed the startled reaction to his question, although he must have.

"What do you mean? You hired me."

"Yes, I hired you. And I still don't understand why you accepted. You aren't like the others. The others each have some problem they're running away from, or at least that's the sense I get. Like they were out of options, and just gave up. I don't get that from you."

"I've got problems," said Bowman, knowing that it sounded silly and defensive. Then he said, "Jesus!" and started with pain as Gordon dabbed at his new stitches with a cotton ball soaked in alcohol.

Gordon laughed. "Relax, my friend. I'm only curious. If you've come to give us what we deserve, you have my blessing. Especially after Esteban killed that cop. But I don't think you're working for the DEA, despite that card Esteban found on Hawk. That's not how they do things."

"What do you mean, 'despite that card'? Hawk had that card, not me."

"I don't see Hawk working with the DEA. It's not how he rolls. He doesn't — he didn't — play well with others. I think he found that card somewhere. And where else but on you, or in your stuff? Is that what set him on you?"

Bowman realized that denial would be useless. He had to take his chances with Gordon. After a moment he said, "Yes. The DEA agent gave me her card when they interrogated me after my arrest." That was true, though certainly misleading. "But I'm not working for them, or anyone else." Also true.

"And you're not here to make some extra cash either. But like I said, more power to you. And I don't need to know. No one can force me to tell what I don't know. Stand up, my friend. Let's look at your legs."

Bowman stood up, and Gordon started by taking the sponge from the bucket and wiping the blood from Bowman's legs. Bowman felt awkward, standing in his underwear while another man washed his legs. But Gordon worked on him with a clinical detachment that communicated itself to Bowman, who soon relaxed.

"So how did you end up here?" Bowman asked. Maybe this was his opening to get Gordon on his side. If he succeeded, the two of them could then approach the others.

"Poor judgment, Archer, and failure of character. After I got out of the service, I didn't know what to do next. I kind of wandered around, staying with different friends in different parts of the country. I started hanging out in sketchy bars on both sides of the border, looking for danger or excitement, I guess. Or maybe trying to hide my shame."

"Hide your shame? What were you ashamed of?" Gordon wanted to talk about it, it seemed, or he wouldn't have brought it up.

"Of being alive, I guess, when so many good men I'd known were not. Sounds crazy, when you say it out loud, but that's how I felt."

"It's not crazy," Bowman said immediately, "and I know just what you mean. But you have to get past it. Your friends who didn't make it back would never have tried to lay that on you. You were just luckier than them, and that's nothing to be ashamed of."

"Yeah, I know that now, but that's how I felt at the time, and it made me reckless, I guess." He frowned and shook his head. After a few moments he continued, "Anyway, El Chato found me, and talked me into joining him. I told myself it was no different than some of the shit I'd done in the service, providing security for some third-world dirt bag that happened to be useful to Uncle Sam for some reason. But it was like Brer Rabbit and the tar baby. I just got pulled in deeper and tighter. And now I'm part of a gang of murderers. I'm sorry I got you mixed up in it. The others too."

"So why don't you just leave? Tell your folks some

story about what you've been doing for the last few months and put this all behind you. Make a new start." After a pause, Bowman added, "And it's not Archer. It's Bowman, Robbie Bowman."

Gordon smiled. "Bowman – Archer. That's funny. My name is Manuel Fuentes. Most people call me Manny. The name 'Gordon' just sort of popped into my head when El Chato asked what to call me. I use to have a dog, an English bulldog we called Gordo, Spanish for Fatty, and it was a play on that. It feels good to let someone else in on the joke." He chuckled. But after a short while his frown returned, and he said, "But we better stick to Archer and Gordon around here."

"Put your weight on your right leg," Gordon said, "while I work on the left. Your right looks fine." After a few moments, he continued, "You asked why I don't just leave. El Chato can't take the risk of me telling what I know. He'd kill me if he caught me trying to leave. I have thought about it, but it's not so easy. El Chato keeps the keys to the trucks. When I do go out, it is always with others, and I am not sure who I can trust. Hawk was the worst, but I'm not entirely sure of the other Americans either, even though I recruited all of them. I don't really trust them, but I also feel responsible for them, and wouldn't feel right about leaving them here without me. But you should go. I wouldn't try to stop you, and I'll help you if I can."

"And how would Chato react to that?"

Gordon shrugged. "He'd probably kill me. He told me to watch you, and make sure you don't have a chance to communicate with anyone. But that's my problem, Robbie, not yours."

None of this was my problem a few days ago, thought Bowman, but he was too far in now to pick and choose his problems. And he liked Gordon. The man refused to make excuses for himself, and was ready to bear the consequences of his actions without complaint.

187

"I can't leave without you, Manny," Bowman said. "I'm gonna need you to take these stitches out." Gordon smiled at that, and Bowman continued, "What about talking to the other Americans? If we were all on the same page, we wouldn't have to be afraid of the Mexicans."

"Let me think about that, Robbie, but I'll need to be cautious. If I confide in the wrong person it could get us both killed. I can feel them out, but it'll take some time."

"I don't think we have much time. This area is crawling with police and DEA, and they'll find us soon enough. If they find Chato while we're still with him, we just have to survive. We might have to do some time, but we didn't kill any cops or sell any drugs." Bowman wasn't sure that the law would be impressed by such distinctions, but it would not be helpful to counsel despair. He didn't want Gordon to think that his only choice was to stick with El Chato, for better or worse. "In the meantime, we look for opportunities."

Gordon had finished bandaging Bowman's wounds, and Bowman carefully dressed in the pants and shirt that Mrs. Flores had given him, the ones that had belonged to her son.

Thank you, Fernando, he thought, they fit perfectly.

CHAPTER 23

El Chato was pacing back and forth in the kitchen of the ranch house, speaking into his mobile phone in Spanish. "I am sorry, amigo, but I cannot make our appointment. We must postpone it."

"How long?" asked the voice on the other end.

"A few days, perhaps a week. I will call you when I am ready."

"You do not have it, do you? You promised me that you had a reliable supply."

"Of course I have it, but I must stay where I am for the time being. The police are looking for me, but in a few days they will settle back into their routine."

The man on the other end of the line was silent for a long time, an uncomfortably long time. Finally, he said, "Ah, yes. I have heard something of this. So that was your doing. You have stirred up a great deal of trouble, amigo, and not just for yourself."

"This trouble will pass, I promise you; just give me some time."

"You have been a good partner, Chato, but I think it is now too dangerous to do business with you. The Federales and the Rurales are all seeking your head. I cannot afford to be nearby when they find it."

"What are you saying, amigo?" El Chato stopped pacing and threw his free hand in the air to emphasize his astonishment and sense of betrayal, a gesture that was wasted on man on the phone. "Have we not both prospered from our relationship?"

"We have, amigo, and I will therefore give you plenty of time. If you are still alive and free in six months, I may reach out to you again. Until then, do not try to contact me." The line went dead.

Mierda! thought El Chato, as he put away his phone. That was one of his best customers. If a few more of his customers came to the same conclusion, he would be out of business. And one could not simply retire from this business. He needed a constant source of cash to pay his people, for without his people he was vulnerable to all of the enemies he had made over the years. Not even Paco and Esteban would stick with him for long if he could not provide for them.

But that was just one customer, and this storm would surely blow over. He had weathered many such storms. Archer had, unwittingly, plugged the leak in his organization by killing Hawk. For a time, he feared that Hawk had told the DEA where they were, but concluded that they would have been here already if he had. Hawk must have been feeding them information a little at a time, and no doubt charging heavily for it. He had been smarter than El Chato had given him credit for. So it was safer to stay here for now; the law would be all over the roads, looking for the black SUVs.

Perhaps Archer could be a replacement for Hawk, someone whom he could trust on his own with special projects, and to watch Gordon and the other gringos. He would watch this Archer closely, and speak to him of this if he seemed like the right choice. Archer would not kill women and children for him, he guessed, but El Chato did not plan on doing any more of that anytime soon. It had been a mistake, caused by his anger. His anger had almost cost him the chance to replace Hawk with Archer as well. He must learn to control it.

CHAPTER 24

It was just after dark, and Bowman, Gordon and Sanborn were playing poker at the little table in the bunkhouse. Bravo Squad was on duty, so it was just the three of them. Three players were not enough for a good game, but a bad game of poker passed the time, at least. Gordon had a little pile of cash that he kept separate from his own money, and he used it for the antes for all three of them.

"This was Ford's," he said. "I don't want to take it for myself, and I can't send it to his folks, 'cause I don't even know what his real name was. So we'll play for it. I think he would've liked that."

"Does it include the pot from the last hand the other night?" Sanborn asked.

"Yes it does, my friend. I would've sworn he was bluffing, but he wasn't."

And then the lights went out.

"Jesus, Mary and Joseph!" Gordon shouted, "Again?"

"Oh no!" moaned Sanborn.

"I think the generator just ran out of gas," Bowman said. "I never got around to filling it this morning, what with Hawk trying to kill me and all."

Gordon and Sanborn relaxed a bit. "Yeah, you're probably right," Gordon said, "but we'd better make an armed reconnaissance."

Gordon found a flashlight, and they all found their rifles. Bowman and Sanborn followed Gordon out of the bunkhouse and they all advanced carefully on the garage. Bravo Squad hadn't noticed the lights going out, since they were outside, but Esteban and Paco appeared at the door to the ranch house, looking nervous. Gordon waved them back and indicated by hand gestures that the three of them would check it out.

A quick scan of the barn showed that no one was in the open area, and they cautiously approached the generator room, rifles up and ready. Gordon signaled for Bowman to kick in the door. Bowman did, and Gordon rushed into the room, followed closely by Sanborn and Bowman.

But Bowman had been right. There was no one in the generator room, except for Hawk's body. Bowman filled the generator's gas tank and restarted it. Then Gordon turned on the single light bulb hanging from the ceiling joist. They'd all avoided the distasteful task of dealing with Hawk's body, and it hadn't been moved in the hours since his death. The bright red blood had dried black, his skin had turned the color of clay, and his eyeballs were drying and shrinking, but otherwise he was just as they'd left him. Bowman's stitches hurt, especially when he moved, but the sight of Hawk's staring eyes and bloody torso put his own problems in perspective. Hawk was the only American that Bowman had ever killed, the only person he'd ever killed outside of a war. Should he feel regret, or something? He didn't. He'd felt much more sympathy for the others he'd killed, for the woman and child in Iraq, of course, but even for the enemy fighters he'd killed. He didn't hate them; they'd been soldiers like him, fighting for a cause that they believed in. But this man had badly needed killing, and the world was a better place without him.

"Who would have thought he had so much blood in him," Sanborn said, as they all looked down at Hawk's corpse.

"Sanborn, you surprise me!" said Gordon, turning to look at him. "You've read Macbeth?"

"What?"

After a beat, Gordon said, "Never mind. My mistake."

"Was this the first time you used that knife?" Sanborn asked, turning to Bowman.

Bowman had used his knife often, as a tool, but he knew what Sanborn meant. He meant used it as a weapon.

"No, it isn't. I had to use it once before, in Afghanistan."

"What happened? Did you run out of ammo?"

Gordon gave Sanborn a sharp, disapproving look, and was about to say something to him, but Bowman stopped him with a look and a slight nod. Sanborn shouldn't have asked questions like that. It is bad manners to put a man in a position where he has to answer questions like that, even to say he doesn't want to talk about it. But Bowman did feel like talking about it. Lately he'd felt like talking about a lot of things. And maybe this would help them gain Sanborn's confidence.

"No, I didn't run out of ammo. We were searching one of those walled compounds that we thought might be an IED factory." IEDs, or Improvised Explosive Devices, were homemade land mines used by the Taliban, and they caused more casualties than any other weapon used by them. Usually they were some kind of artillery or mortar round rigged to explode when driven over, or when triggered by remote radio command. "There was a family there, a woman, a couple of kids and one man. He looked like he was about fifty years old, but he was probably only about thirty or thirty-five."

"I know what you mean," Gordon said. "Something about the way they live seems to put a lot of mileage on them."

"So we put the family in a small room and I was told to watch them while the others searched the place. They weren't exactly happy to see us, but they were cooperative enough. I got careless."

"The guy jumped you?" Sanborn said.

"He grabbed the barrel of my rifle and rushed me."

"A guy tried that with me once," said Gordon.

"So what happened," said Sanborn, turning his attention to Gordon.

"I shot him. It's not a very interesting story. Go on, Archer. I'm guessing you weren't able to shoot your guy."

"No, I wasn't. By the time I realized what was going on my rifle wasn't pointed at him anymore. I managed to hang on to the grip with my right hand, but he had two hands on it and it was pointing to my left and sandwiched between us. The guy kept coming and pushing me back, and I stumbled over something and fell backwards, with him on top of me."

Bowman remembered the look of hate on the man's face, inches from his own. He remembered the rank smell of his hot breath, his yellow teeth and his black, greasy beard. He remembered his surprise at how strong the man was. Bowman was bigger and younger, but the man's strength was at least a match for his own. He remembered the feeling of desperation and humiliation. Here he was, fully armed and in full battle rattle, about to be killed by an unarmed old man.

"So I gather you went for your knife," Sanborn said, "but why not go for your pistol instead?"

"That was my first thought, but I couldn't get at my pistol without letting go of my rifle. I'd have the pistol, but he'd have the rifle, and I wasn't sure who would be able to shoot first. At that point, I think I'd actually forgotten I had the knife. And while I was trying to decide what to do, the son of a bitch head butts me right in the face."

"Ouch!" said Sanborn. Gordon winced in sympathy.

"So now I've got a smashed nose and a busted lip, and I was starting to choke on my own blood, lying on my back like that. Then I feel him working one of his hands towards my pistol. I twisted my body to try to get it on top of my pistol, so he couldn't get at it, but I was starting to think that this would not end well."

"And then you remembered your knife?" Gordon asked.

"Yes. My left hand was free, and I reached down, pulled the blade and buried it up to the hilt in the side of his neck. I must have hit the brain stem or something, because he didn't even take the time to bleed out, but just died instantly, right on top of me."

"Wow," said Sanborn. "I hope they gave you the rest of the day off."

Bowman smiled weakly at Sanborn's jest, but he was thinking about what, at least in his memory, had been the worst part of the whole episode. *What the hell, I might as well get it out there, while I'm in the mood to talk.*

"So I rolled the guy's body off of me and I realized that his wife and kids had been watching the whole thing."

"Damn!" Sanborn said.

Gordon looked down at his feet and said nothing.

They were all silent for a long time. Finally, Gordon pointed down at Hawk's body and, looking at Bowman, said, "You want his tomahawk? I'd say you earned it. 'To the victor goes the spoils,' as they say."

"No, I don't want it," said Bowman. "I think it's been used in some evil deeds. We should bury the hatchet with its owner."

"It's a tomahawk, not a hatchet," said Sanborn.

"I stand corrected," said Bowman.

Gordon smiled and rolled his eyes a little, so only Bowman could see, and then said, "You think he killed that woman and child in Tierra Roja?"

"I do," said Bowman.

"Yeah, I guess I had come to the same conclusion," Gordon said. "He had the opportunity, and I believe he would've been capable of it. But why? Just for yucks?"

"After I was arrested, the police told me that the victims were the wife and daughter of a DEA agent named Walker, and they thought El Chato had them killed as revenge for some busted drug deal that Walker was responsible for."

Both Gordon and Sanborn visibly jerked, and Bowman thought he could almost hear the pieces clicking into place in their brains. Gordon recovered quickly, but Sanborn was wide-eyed and pale. That was a good sign.

"We're in up to our necks with some very bad people with some powerful enemies," Bowman said, looking particularly at Sanborn. "We need to stick together if we want to get out of this with all our parts. What do you say, Sanborn, will you follow our lead if we find a way to get ourselves out of this mess?"

Sanborn nodded slowly, and said nothing for a while. Finally, he gathered himself together and said, "Yes, I'm in with whatever you guys come up with. Just don't leave me here on my own."

"We won't," said Bowman. "We'll talk to the others as soon as we get the chance. Once we're all on board, we can stand up to the Mexicans. In the meantime, don't say anything to anyone. We don't know yet who we can trust."

"I'm sorry I got you into this, Sanborn," Gordon said, "but stick with Archer and me and we'll get you out of it. In the meantime, try to act normally. Tomorrow morning, take Carter and go bury Hawk out where we buried the three from the other day. We haven't spoken to Carter yet, so watch what you say to him. And bury Hawk's tomahawk with him."

CHAPTER 25

"According to my source, this is the layout of the Rocking H Ranch, or was sixty years or so ago."

Cane handed out copies of his rough sketch to the law enforcement officers assembled in the half-light just before dawn. Most of them were members of the State Police Tactical Team, sixteen of them in an MRAP, or Mine Resistant Ambush Protected troop carrier, and four SUVs, each wearing a helmet and body armor and carrying an M4 assault rifle. Cane himself represented the Bronco County Sheriff's Department. The Drug Enforcement Administration was represented by Clementine Bates, who rode with Cane. They'd borrowed helmets and body armor from the State Police, but didn't carry rifles. Their vehicles were parked on both sides of the main road, at the entrance to the long access road, or track, that led to the ranch. The deputy he'd posted here overnight had seen no one coming or going while he was here, so if El Chato and his people were at the ranch last night, they'd be there this morning.

A State Police captain named McGuire was in charge, since this was a State Police operation, but Sheriff Cane had better information and a personal interest in this, so

McGuire was willing to defer to him for now.

"It's about two miles or so down this track," Cane said to the group, "and this is the only easy way in or out. I'm not sure how much Captain McGuire has told you already, so I'll recap. We have reason to believe that El Chato and his people are holed up at the ranch, and that they are responsible for at least three murders: A Sheriff's deputy, who was a personal friend of mine, and a young woman and a little girl, the wife and daughter of a DEA agent named Walker, who is a colleague of Agent Bates here. They shot Walker, too, and he's fighting for his life right now. So these are some mean hombres, and should be approached as such. Deputy Abbott was killed with a submachine gun, and a man that witnessed the shooting of Agent Walker told us that at least several of them carry military-style assault rifles and are familiar with military infantry tactics. According to this witness, there are about ten of them. That witness may be with them now, and we think he's friendly."

Cane surveyed the assembled armada. This was a formidable force of well trained, well armed men. The easy thing would be to go in with guns blazing, and take no prisoners. But they had to resist the temptation, and not just because Bowman was there. This wasn't a war, and if it ever became a war it would give the bad guys more legitimacy than they deserved. These were criminals, not soldiers, and should be treated as such.

"Don't let this armored truck and these helmets and assault rifles fool you into thinking this is a military operation," he said. "We're cops, and we're here to take these people into custody. That's what all of the empty seats are for. I don't think we'll run into more than we can handle, but if we do we hold them in place and call for help. No heroes, please."

Cane thought that was enough. Too much planning, or too-detailed instructions, would be counterproductive, given how little they knew about what to expect. They would have to react as best they could to whatever they found.

"Captain McGuire, anything you want to add?"

"I think you covered most of it, Sheriff. The plan is to spread out as we get in sight of the ranch, as the terrain allows, with this bad boy in the center," he said, pointing at the MRAP. "We have a chopper dedicated to this operation, to give us an eye in the sky and track anyone that tries to run away across country, but we've asked them to stay out of sight and earshot until we're on scene. We want to take them by surprise. You should tune your radios to channel six and listen for any instructions as we get closer."

At that, and just as the morning sun peaked over the eastern horizon, they all climbed into their vehicles and the convoy moved off, led by the MRAP. After the end of the Iraq war, the Pentagon had declared hundreds of them surplus and given them away to various law enforcement agencies. The New Mexico State Police had gotten two. It was armored all around, with bullet-proof glass, and weighed eighteen tons, but could reach speeds of sixty-five miles per hour. The machine gun turret had been closed up and it had been painted a matte black, but otherwise it was the same as the military used in Iraq and Afghanistan. Cane thought that they could probably drive that thing right through any of the ranch buildings, if they had to. It was intimidating, and he was glad they'd brought it along.

Cane drove one of the Sheriff Department's Ford Explorer SUVs. He usually preferred his old Crown Vic, but the Explorer was better off road. That old Crown Vic represented a different era, Cane thought, my era. Ford had discontinued it in 2011, so the one he had would be his last, which was a shame. But he was glad he had the SUV now.

The track to the ranch – 'road' was too grand a term – was rocky, rough and circuitous, and the going was slow. Occasionally, they'd dip into a dry wash, crawl over a dry creek bed and clamber up the far side. Cane had to keep his jaw clenched to avoid biting his tongue as they bounced over the rough ground. Bates was holding tight to the handle above her door.

"So he did it, even after I told him not to?" said Bates.

Cane gave her a quick sideways look and smiled, before turning his eyes back to the track. "Looks that way, miss. Some men just don't listen."

"I'd hate to see him get hurt."

"So would I," Cane said. And that was true, but he thought he detected in her tone something more than what Cane himself meant. Well don't that beat all, he thought. Agent Clementine Bates seems to have a personal interest in citizen Robbie Bowman's safety.

They'd driven about half way to the ranch when a black SUV suddenly emerged from around a curve in the track and nearly collided head on with the MRAP leading the convoy. The SUV had been screened by a rock outcropping, so that by the time they saw it, and whoever was in the SUV saw the police convoy, it was already upon them. The SUV came to a sudden stop just feet from the front of the MRAP and almost immediately started to move in reverse, but Cane quickly pulled his vehicle around the MRAP, past the black SUV and angled it across the track behind it, effectively blocking it in. The State Police vehicles also moved around the MRAP, and the black SUV was soon surrounded. In seconds Cane and Bates, as well as the entire Tactical Team, were training their weapons over their vehicles at the men in the black SUV.

McGuire sent one of his units down the track a bit, to cover their flank and make sure that there wasn't another vehicle behind this one, then shouted, "Out of the car with your hands up! Do it now!"

The passengers of the SUV hesitated only briefly, and then front doors opened and two men stepped out, their hands in the air.

The Tactical Team quickly converged from three sides, their rifles at ready, and the two men were soon spread-eagled and leaning against their SUV. They were unarmed, but otherwise matched Bowman's general description of the security team at the old silver mine, Cane thought. They were on the right track.

As soon as they were searched and handcuffed, McGuire walked over to Cane and Bates and said, "How about you see what you can learn from these two about what's ahead, while we search the SUV?"

"Of course, Captain," said Bates. To Cane she said, "We should probably split them up for this, so they can't take cues from each other. Which one do you want?"

Cane looked at the two men, now standing near the hood of their SUV, their hands cuffed behind them. One of them, the one in the lighter shirt, look sullen and angry. The other, in the darker shirt, looked nervous and scared.

"I'll take the fella in the dark shirt," he said.

"I was afraid you were going to say that," she sighed.

They started towards the two men, but were soon stopped by a shout from McGuire.

"Cane, Bates, you're gonna wanna see this. They've got a dead body in the back! Doesn't look like he died in his sleep, either."

Cane felt sick, and he saw that Clementine Bates had suddenly gotten a shade paler. Bowman?

"We don't need to both look, miss. Why don't you keep an eye on these two desperados while I go see if — if it's anyone we know."

"Thank you, Sheriff," she said weakly. "I'll just — I'll just wait here then."

Cane walked over to McGuire, who was standing at the open hatch at the back of the black SUV. The body had been wrapped loosely in an old tarpaulin, which McGuire had pulled aside. It was not Bowman. He said, loud enough for Clementine Bates to hear, but not looking in her direction, "No one I've ever seen before."

Then he bent over and looked more closely. McGuire had been right. This man had not died in his sleep. Unless someone had gutted him while he slept. And he hadn't died recently. From the look of it, he had been dead several hours, maybe as much as a day. And there was some kind of a two-headed hatchet lying next to the body. The weapon he was killed with? Could've been. It was certainly a messy job.

Straightening up, he said to McGuire, "I'll go see what his two friends can tell us about this."

When he rejoined Clementine Bates, he saw that she had regained her color, and was looking a little sheepish.

"I'm sorry, Sheriff. I guess I was just — I mean I should've . . ."

Cane interrupted her before she could go on, "Don't know what you're talking about, miss. Why don't you take your man over yonder a piece and see what he has to say, while I talk to his friend here."

Bates gave him a grateful look, then walked up to the surly man in the lighter shirt.

"Walk this way, sir. You and I are going to have a little chat."

"Fuck you, bitch. I don't gotta talk to you."

She didn't reply, but reached around behind his back and squeezed one of his handcuffs tighter.

"Ow! Goddamn bitch! You can't do that, it's police brutality!" He looked around for support, but all the cops in vicinity were studiously ignoring him and trying to suppress smiles.

"I think that other cuff may be a little loose as well. Shall I check?" she said.

"No, please! I'll walk, but I don't gotta say nothing."

"A man who knows his rights. I am very impressed," she said, sounding unimpressed, then took his arm and lead him away.

Well done, thought Cane. She can be a hard ass when she needs to be. When they were gone, Cane sized up the other man. He looked even more nervous and scared than he had at first, almost in a panic. Cane did not read him his Miranda rights. What he needed now was operational intelligence, and he was prepared to accept that his statements couldn't be used against him in court.

"I expect you boys come from the ranch up yonder," said Cane, motioning with his thumb up the track.

"Yes, sir, but we just provide security. We don't get involved in none of the shit they're up to. I had no idea they was murdering people. Women and children, even. I swear, I had no idea." He was sweating heavily, and shifting his weight constantly from one foot to the other.

"I believe you, son. You were working for El Chato, but didn't know about all the bad stuff he was up to."

"Yeah, that's right. Exactly. I've been lookin' for a way out," he said, bobbing his head up and down enthusiastically.

Bingo! thought Cane. This is the place, all right. He said, "Well, you're out now, son. We'll sort out what you did or didn't know or do soon enough. What I need to know right now is how many are at that ranch and how they're armed. The more you cooperate now, while it's useful, the friendlier we'll be in the future."

"I'm your man, Sheriff. My name is Sanborn, Pete Sanborn. That's my real name. The other guy calls himself Carter, but I don't think that's his real name. Just remember, Sheriff, the helpful guy was Pete Sanborn."

"I'll remember that, Sanborn. Now tell me how many are left at the ranch, and what kind of arms they're carrying."

"Will do, Sheriff. Let's see, there's Chato and the other two Mexicans, and there's seven of us in the security detail," he said. "Six, I mean," he added, looking a little uncomfortable.

"The seventh was the guy in the tarp?"

"Yes. But I didn't kill him." His eyes were pleading with Cane to believe him.

"We'll get to that in a minute. So four in the security detail, not counting you and your friend Carter?"

"Yes, sir. But he ain't my friend."

"Is one of those four named Bowman?"

"Bowman? No, nobody called Bowman."

"What kinds of weapons are they carrying?"

"Well, we mostly carry pistols and civilian versions of the M4. Nothing illegal. But Esteban's got an H&K UMP9. Know what that is? I don't think that's legal." Sanborn was starting to relax a little, and stopped the constant shifting of his weight from side to side.

"Yes, I know what that is." It was the submachine gun that killed Abbott. Esteban just moved up Cane's most wanted list.

Cane pulled a copy of his father's hand-drawn map from his shirt pocket, unfolded it, and showed it to Sanborn. "Is this an accurate map of the ranch?"

Sanborn studied the map, turning it one way or another from time to time. "Pretty close," he said. "The scale is a little off. The buildings should be smaller or farther apart. But yeah, pretty close."

Good memory, Dad, thought Cane. To Sanborn, he said, "So what's in those buildings now?"

"El Chato and his Mexicans live in the ranch house, here," he said, pointing at the map, "and the rest of us are in the bunk house, here. That's the garage, which used to be a barn, I guess."

"Tell me about the dead man."

"I didn't kill him. I wasn't even there when it happened." The pleading eyes again.

"I believe you, son. Who was he?"

"Called himself Hawk, but I don't think it was his real name."

"So who killed Hawk, and why?" Cane asked.

"It was some kind of a knife fight, a personal grudge thing. Guy that killed him was a new guy, calls himself Archer. Archer was the one that told me about the murder of the woman and child. Said he thought Hawk did it. He was gonna help me get out."

Archer, Cane thought, and smiled to himself.

Clementine Bates came back with Carter. She'd loosened the cuff, once she'd made her point, but hadn't learned much from him. That wasn't her fault, Cane thought. He didn't think he'd have done any better with Carter. For whatever reason, Sanborn had been eager to talk and Carter had not.

Cane filled Bates and McGuire in on what he'd learned, and the convoy rolled on.

CHAPTER 26

Bowman and Gordon walked out of the bunk house in the early morning light. They were preparing to relieve Samson and Blake, who had been on sentry duty most of the night. Samson was standing in the middle of the courtyard, by the well, and Blake was stationed on the far side of the corral, out of sight. Sanborn and Carter had gone to bury Hawk. Esteban was on the ramada of the ranch house, leaning against one of the support posts, his submachine gun slung in front of him. This put Samson and Esteban to the left of Bowman and Gordon as they emerged from the bunk house, Samson about fifty feet away and Esteban about one hundred.

"Holy Shit!" Samson shouted, looking towards the gate and the access road. Whatever Samson had seen was screened from Bowman and Gordon by the bunk house, but Esteban saw it too and stepped away from the post, gripping his submachine gun tightly. Samson started to bring his M4 up to bear on whatever he'd seen, hesitated for a moment, then tossed his rifle aside and started running to his left, across the front of Bowman and Gordon.

Esteban, who'd been facing the gate, saw Samson

running out of the corner of his eye. With his lumbering gate, he hadn't gotten far before Esteban turned, brought his gun up and fired a burst into Samson's back. Samson's arms flew up as he fell to his knees, his mouth open in a silent scream. Then he fell forward on his face, in widening pool of blood. His right leg twitched for a moment, and then he was still.

Bowman and Gordon stood for a moment frozen in shock and then, almost as one, they brought their M4s up and began firing at Esteban. They were disciplined shots, aimed at center mass. Esteban seemed surprised by this return fire, and he was hit at least twice before he realized what was happening. Heavier rounds might have knocked him over, but the 5.56 millimeter rounds fired by the M4s did not. They passed right through him and punched holes in the ranch house wall behind him, followed almost instantaneously by blood sprays that painted the wall a bright red. Esteban had only moments to live, but time enough to pivot the few degrees needed to target Bowman and Gordon and fire a long burst before he crumpled to the floor boards of the ramada with six holes in his chest and six matching, larger holes in his back.

Most of the rounds from Esteban's final burst had gone wild, but one had hit Bowman in the upper right arm and twisted him to his right. There was no pain yet, just a jolt, but his right arm was suddenly lifeless and his rifle fell from his grasp and clattered into the dust at his feet. The impact had turned him towards Gordon, and he saw that he had been hit as well, because he was lying face down in the dust. Bowman dropped to his knees beside Gordon and used his left arm to roll him over on his back. Bowman saw an entry wound on his left side and a bloody crease on the left side of his head. He was breathing, though shallowly, and there was no blood on his lips.

Gordon is dead, thought Bowman. He had died the moment that he'd stood with Bowman against Esteban. Gordon was dead, but Manuel Fuentes lived, at least for now. Don't leave me Manny, please don't leave me.

But there was no time now for either hope or despair. The ground around them began to erupt in gouts of earth, and Bowman looked up to see El Chato running towards them and firing his pistol. He must have come out to see what was happening and decided to finish what Esteban had started. Bowman now registered the sound of El Chato's pistol and of another weapon, a rifle by the sound of it, being fired inside the ranch house. Paco was inside, and was firing at someone or something through one of the windows. Probably at whatever Samson and Esteban had seen, but Bowman had no time to consider what that might be.

Bowman threw himself to his left and started rolling. He wanted to present a moving target to El Chato, and to draw his fire away from Fuentes. As he rolled, he struggled to get his left hand over to his right hip, where his Beretta was holstered. And now the pain came, as he rolled over his injured right arm and the recent wounds from his fight with Hawk. The pain was like a dull roar, except when he rolled onto the arm, when it became sharp and stabbing, and he thought he might pass out. El Chato's rounds were not all missing. Bowman could feel the impacts, but if there was pain from those injuries it was lost in the general mix, the dull roar that was growing into an insane scream. And none of the new injuries were disabling, which was all that Bowman could care about for now.

He soon realized that the only position from which he could get at the pistol on his right hip with his left hand was on his back, so he stopped rolling. As soon as his left hand found his Beretta, he pulled it free from its holster. He put in on his stomach and twisted it around until he could get a proper grip on it with his left hand. Had he already chambered a round? He didn't think he could work the slide with only one good arm, so he could only hope that he had. As soon as he got a good grip, he straightened his arm in front of his head and began firing as fast as he could.

On his back, he couldn't see where he was shooting, only the pale blue sky above, but he hoped that it was in the general direction of El Chato. He had decided that it was more important to return fire quickly than to reposition himself for a better aim. He could only hope it was the right choice.

After what seemed like an eternity, but must have been mere seconds, he became aware that El Chato was no longer firing at him, and he rolled over onto his stomach to see how well he'd done. El Chato was on his knees, sitting back on his heels, no more than twenty feet from him. His pistol was in his lap. His left arm hung useless, and Bowman could see at least two bright red blooms on his white shirt front. El Chato was struggling to load a new magazine into his pistol with his one good hand. Bowman thought that he'd done well, considering that he'd been shooting blindly. It looked like it would only take a few more seconds for El Chato to finish reloading, but that was plenty of time. From twenty feet, he couldn't miss, and one more well aimed round should be enough to finish El Chato. He raised the Beretta, but his vision was blurring, and he couldn't hold it steady. Focus, he told himself, we're almost done. With an effort, he steadied his gun, took careful aim at El Chato's chest and squeezed the trigger.

Nothing.

He saw now what he should've seen at once; the Beretta's slide was retracted and locked. He'd fired all fifteen rounds while on his back. Maybe he should've chosen the Glock, with its seventeen-round magazine, he thought, and his heart sank. His strength was gone, and the empty pistol slipped out of his hand as he watched El Chato finish loading the new magazine and take slow, careful aim at his head.

"Pendejo!" El Chato spat, and then the side of his head

exploded.

Bowman's vision was swimming, and he was being tossed about in a sea of pain. He struggled to understand what was happening. Was that his own head that he'd seen erupt in a geyser of blood, brains and bone? Was he a disembodied spirit floating above all this, witnessing his own death? He'd heard of such things. No, he decided, it hurt too much for that. He looked to his right and saw that Fuentes was now on his stomach, both arms in front of him and holding his pistol. He was looking over at Bowman, and smiled weakly. And then Bowman surrendered to the raging sea and was carried away into the dark.

CHAPTER 27

The darkness took him in and showed him a series of scenes from his life, beginning with recent events and progressing backward in time. Some of them were brief, almost snapshots. Others were long and involved. He was at once inside the scenes and outside them, inside as an actor, with all the feelings and thoughts appropriate to the time and place, and outside as an observer in the here and now.

There were scenes from Iraq and Afghanistan, of course, some horrific, but not all. Boone was there, as were Ace and Murphy and others. The Bowman inside the scenes felt as he had felt at the time, happy, anguished, bored, angry, afraid. The Bowman outside the scenes watched and reflected. Sometimes he approved of how his younger self had acted or felt. Other times he did not. Sometimes he was proud of himself. Too often he was ashamed. Of things he did or said, and shouldn't have. Of things he did not do or say, and should have.

Each scene was followed by another from an earlier time in his life. After the wars came high school, his parents, his friends, Bridget. The night he lost his virginity, his first kiss, skinny dipping with his friends at the old quarry, Christmas mornings, snowball fights. He recognized the progression backward in time, and he wondered what would happen when he reached the end, or rather the beginning, and there was no more life left to relive. The last scene was one of his earliest memories.

Reggie's a stupid name for a dog, thought Robbie. Robbie's older sister, Bridget, had named him, and he was really her dog. Reggie was part Beagle, like Snoopy, and part every other kind of dog, and he was no fun. He didn't sit on top of his dog house and fight the Red Baron, or even chase squirrels, or play catch. Bridget said he used to, but now he was old. All he did was lie around the house, always near Bridget. And lately he had started having accidents in the house, and he smelled bad.

Robbie asked his dad if he could get a new dog, a puppy that he could name Bandit or Scout, or something else that was a good name for a dog. Bandit would play catch, chase cars, dig up the yard, and do all the things that a proper dog was supposed to do.

Dad said that Reggie might not like having another dog in the house, especially a puppy, but he also said that he didn't think that Reggie would be with them much longer. We'll get you a puppy after Reggie is gone, he said.

Robbie could hardly wait. A dog of his own!

Reggie slept on Bridget's bed, but couldn't get up or down by himself anymore. Sometimes he needed to go outside at night to pee, and Bridget would have to get up to help him down, let him out, and put him back up on her bed when he was done. It seemed like a big nuisance to Robbie, but Bridget didn't seem to mind.

One night, Robbie was awoken by a loud thump, followed quickly by a frantic yell from Bridget, calling for Mom and Dad. They all converged on Bridget's room, where Reggie lay on the floor panting, his legs splayed out to the sides.

Bridget was on her knees next to Reggie, stroking his head. "He tried to get down by himself," Bridget sobbed.

"I would have helped him!" After a little, she continued, "He can't get up, Dad, we need to take him to the vet!"

"It's the middle of the night, Sweetie. We'll take him in the morning if he's not better by then." As Dad said this, he looked over at Mom, with a strange look on his face. Bridget didn't see it, but Robbie did. There was something he didn't want to say out loud.

"Look, he's getting up!" Bridget exclaimed.

And he was. Reggie got to his feet and slowly started for the front door, a little wobbly, but determined. At the door, he stopped, waiting for Bridget to open the door for him. As she did, she turned to the others, who were following behind, and smiled through her drying tears. "He's all better!"

When Bridget couldn't see, Dad gave Mom that look again.

Reggie walked outside, but instead of lifting his leg and 'taking care of business,' as Dad liked to say, he just walked about six feet out into the yard and lay down.

"Get up, Reggie!" Bridget said, and started to cry again.

"He can't, Sweetie," Dad said, and he stooped down, gathered Reggie in his arms and took him back into the house, where he laid him in one of his doggie beds.

Bridget sat down on the floor next to Reggie, stroking his head and softly crying. The rest of them stood around, being sad. In a few minutes, Reggie shuddered, stiffened, and then relaxed. His tongue was hanging out and his eyes were open, but he wasn't panting anymore.

Dad put his hand on Bridget's shoulder and said, "He's gone, Sweetie. I'm sorry."

Bridget got up from the floor, wrapped her arms around Dad's waist, buried her face in his stomach and cried like Robbie had never seen her cry before. Dad patted Bridget's head and Mom put her hand on her shoulder, but neither said anything.

It was then, with horror, that Robbie realized what he had done. He had wished for this, and it had happened.

"I'm sorry, Bridget!" he cried, and wrapped his arms around her waist, just as she had wrapped hers around Dad's. It was a daisy chain of hugs that lasted for only a moment, for Bridget turned from being comforted to comforting Robbie, stroking his hair and saying, "It's OK, Robbie, it's OK."

But it wasn't OK.

After the last scene there was only blackness. Bowman felt like he was floating in the middle of a dark cave. He couldn't see the walls of the cave – he couldn't see anything – but he could sense them, and they were moving. At times they were close, so close that he thought he would be crushed, and at other times they moved farther away and the pressure eased. He was neither cold nor hot, neither wet nor dry. There was no pain. He could feel nothing, see nothing and smell nothing. And he could hear nothing except the voices.

The voices would fade in and out. Sometimes he could hear them clearly, and at other times they seemed far away. He recognized the voices. His mother's first. She was talking to him, he knew. He could understand individual words, but couldn't connect them into anything meaningful. But it didn't matter, because he could tell by her tone that all was well. He wanted to reply, but couldn't. But she understood, and all was well.

Soon his father's voice joined his mother's. His voice was firmer, not quite so sweet, but strong and reassuring. The two voices harmonized beautifully, exactly an octave apart. Again, he could make out words, but no meaning beyond love and reassurance.

Boone's voice was soon added, like a melody played against a bass line. The tone of Boone's voice was more playful than reassuring. He too seemed to understand that Robbie couldn't reply, and he didn't mind.

Bridget's voice was missing, and he felt its absence. But it seemed right and proper and good that it was missing. She was not where they were.

The symphony of voices played for a long time, and seemed to become clearer and louder the closer the walls came, and to fade as the walls receded. Finally, the walls receded and did not come back, and the beautiful voices faded away with them.

For a long time there was nothing, and then he heard new voices. These voices didn't have the same musical quality, but he was happy to hear them. They came and went. Sometimes there was only one, and sometimes there were a few. Sometimes they seemed to be talking to him, but mostly they were not. Some of the voices he recognized, and some he didn't. He recognized the voices of Sheriff Cane, of Mrs. Flores, and of Manny.

As before, he could make out individual words, but couldn't put them together, until the words in the voice of Mrs. Flores started to form patterns that he recognized at some deep level. He recognized the patterns from his childhood. He hadn't heard those patterns much in recent years, but he'd heard them over and over again as a child, and he recognized them now. The recognition allowed him to put meaning to those words.

"Hail Mary, full of grace . . . Our Father, who art in heaven . . . deliver us from evil . . . forgive us our trespasses . . . forgive us our trespasses . . ."

The voices came and went, and they were absent when the darkness of the cave relented and the light began to grow. There were no voices then, but he heard other sounds, the hum and beeping of electronic equipment and the whir of a fan. He felt stiff sheets and smelled disinfectant, and he was thirsty.

CHAPTER 28

"You didn't leave much for us to do, son," Cane said, smiling. He was sitting at the side of Bowman's bed, his hat in his hands. Mrs. Flores was there too, next to Cane. "I told you about the two we picked up on the way in. The Mexican guy in the ranch house made the mistake of firing at us and was shot dead pretty quick. The walls of that old ranch house let in a lot more light now than they used to. The guy you called Blake surrendered without a fuss. We found you and Fuentes and got you both on the chopper right away. Fuentes might have survived the drive out of there, but you wouldn't have. It was touch and go as it was."

"You nearly died, Robbie," Mrs. Flores said, looking troubled by the memory of that close call, even now that he was safe. She was dressed in what Bowman guessed was her Sunday best, a floral print dress and a straw hat with artificial flowers decorating the hat band. Was today Sunday? He had no idea.

"I'm glad I didn't," Bowman said. "Thank you for your concern, ma'am, and for coming to visit me."

Mrs. Flores smiled, as if she'd just been awarded a prize. A little appreciation goes a long way, thought

Bowman.

That exchange seemed to remind Cane of something, and he said, "Detective Carrillo sends his regards. He'd be here himself, but he's out of State on some sort of special project."

"That's unusual, isn't it, for a homicide detective to have to go out of State?"

"I thought so, too. He didn't want to talk about where he was or what he was doing. The man does not indulge in a lot of small talk. But he asked about you, and said he'd come see you when he gets back. In the meantime, he sends his regards."

Bowman nodded and, after a moment, said, "So what's going to happen to Blake and the others?"

"Well, I expect they'll be able to plead down to some minimal time, probably be out in six months or so. They aren't angels, but they're mostly just stupid, not evil."

Bowman was glad to hear that they'd all have second chances. "What about Fuentes? They told me he's been up and about for a while now."

"Well now, he's a special case. The DA can't decide whether to throw him in jail or give him a medal. I expect he'll call it even and just let him walk. He did come through for us at the end."

"Yes he did, Sheriff. He's a good man." Bowman was silent for a few moments. Manny will be all right, then, he thought, and he was pleased. "Sheriff, I know you have to put something out to the press, but if you can try to emphasize in his case the way it ended, rather than what came before, I'd appreciate it. Fuentes has family in Miami, and I think he's worried about what they'll think."

"That speaks well of him," Cane said. "I'll do what I can."

"Thank you, Sheriff. And what about Walker? Is he OK?"

"Yes, he's fine. He didn't remember anything about what happened to him, or what happened to his wife and daughter. I hear that's not uncommon with head injuries. They had to tell him all over again. I'm glad that wasn't my job. Apart from that, there's no sign of brain damage. He should be fine – physically."

They all thought about that in silence for a while. Having lost Boone and his parents, Bowman thought he probably knew better than most what Walker must be going through, and he wished him well.

Finally, Bowman said, "I saw El Chato shoot Walker, I saw Esteban kill Abbott, and I'll swear on a stack of bibles that Hawk killed Mrs. Walker and their little girl. He pretty much admitted it, but is the DA convinced of that?"

"He is, son, and those files are closed. Fuentes and the others backed you up on Walker and Abbott, and the ballistics evidence confirms it. Hawk's tomahawk is consistent with the wounds on his victims, and they found a strand of hair in the sink at the murder scene that was consistent with his, as well as some footprints that match his boots. Turns out he was discharged from the Army a couple of years ago for 'personality disorder.' I'd say they got that right. Want to know what Hawk's real name was?"

"No, Sheriff, not really." A real name would make him seem more human, Bowman thought, and he had no interest in humanizing Hawk. He had no regrets about killing Hawk, but he didn't want to know anything more about him.

"Yeah, I guess it doesn't really matter, does it?"

In the silence that followed this, Mrs. Flores said, "I prayed for you, Robbie."

"Yes, ma'am, I know. I heard you."

"You did?" She was almost bursting with happiness. "I am so glad. And I think God heard me too."

"You mean because I survived?"

"Partly, yes, but mostly because your eyes have changed."

"They're still kind, I hope."

"Yes, Robbie, they are still kind. But now, I think, they are not so sad."

CHAPTER 29

Manny came the next day. A few of the tubes and machines had been removed, and Bowman was able to sit up in bed and eat now.

"You're looking good, Manny. I like the new part in your hair."

Fuentes grinned. "I may need to wear it a little longer from now on. How are you doing, Robbie? You look a lot better than last time I saw you at the ranch."

Bowman laughed. "I'll bet. They tell me I should make a full recovery." He turned serious then. "But it wouldn't have gone as well for me if El Chato had gotten off one more shot. Thank you, Manny."

Fuentes looked uncomfortable. "Now don't start that, please. He'd have killed us both if not for what you did. And I owe you more than I can say. You gave me a chance to earn back some self-respect."

"And you took it, Manny. You took that chance, and you came through when it mattered." Fuentes looked at his feet and said nothing, but Bowman could tell that he was pleased, if a little embarrassed. That was more than enough of the heart-to-heart talk. "So what are you going to do now?"

Manny seemed relieved by the change of topic. "Well, I've been cooperating with the police, and I think they're going to let me off without any charges. That's more than I deserve, but I'm pleased that it's worked out so well. As soon as they let me, I plan to go home, to Miami. I'll try to regain the respect of my family and find something useful to do with my life."

Bowman thought that Fuentes was probably not giving his family as much credit as they deserved, and that regaining their respect, if he'd ever lost it, would not be difficult. But maybe it was better to go in expecting the worst. As for finding something useful to do with his life, that cut close to home for Bowman. What had he himself been doing over the last year or so that had been useful, apart from this latest little adventure? But he did feel, like Fuentes, that he'd earned back at least some part of something that he'd lost. He'd filled a hole in his soul. And Mrs. Flores had seen it in his eyes.

Fuentes noticed Bowman's copy of Moby Dick on the table by the bed, and said, "So did you finish it?"

"Yes, I did, and the story does pick up towards the end, after the treatise on whaling. You want to give it another try?"

Fuentes smiled. "Yes, I think I will," he said, and picked up the book. "Thanks. But there's a letter in it."

"Yes. Would you mind mailing it for me?"

"Sure," Fuentes said as he pulled the letter from the book. His fingers happened upon the small, hard object in the letter. He looked quickly at Bowman's neck and saw that the little gold Jesus was gone. He glanced at the address and said, "His mother?"

"Yes. I never should have taken it."

"I think she'll understand. And be happy to have it."

"I hope so," Bowman said. After a few moments, he continued, "I'll come visit you, Manny, when I'm back on my feet."

"I hope you do, Robbie," Fuentes said, and looked like

he meant it.

Detective Carrillo came in as Fuentes was leaving, and they exchanged brief nods as they passed each other. Bowman was surprised to see him so soon. Cane had said he was out of state somewhere just the other day.

"You look well, Mr. Bowman. I am happy to see it." As usual, Carrillo was dressed impeccably, in a light gray silk suit, yellow tie and matching pocket square.

"Thanks for coming, Detective. Have a seat." Bowman was happy to see Carrillo. He was an easy man to like, although probably not an easy man to get to know well.

Carrillo remained standing at the foot of the bed at parade rest, his arms crossed behind him. "Thank you, but I cannot stay long. I have something to tell you."

That didn't sound good. He could read nothing from Carrillo's face, but 'I have something to tell you' is usually followed by bad news.

"Go on."

"While you were — sleeping — I made some inquiries, which I hope you will not find presumptuous of me." Carrillo paused for a beat, then added, "I may have found your sister, Bridget."

Bowman's jaw dropped, and he stared open-mouthed at Carrillo. Before he could speak, Carrillo continued.

"I say may have, Mr. Bowman. I did not speak to the woman. That would have been — an intrusion. And she knows nothing of my inquiries. But I have good reason to believe that this woman is your sister." As Carrillo said this, he walked around to the side of the bed, fished a small piece of note paper from an inside pocket of his suit jacket and handed it to Bowman.

Bowman's hand shook as he took the paper. On it Carrillo had written a name and address in a neat, almost feminine hand. Bowman did not recognize the name. The address was in Oregon. Bowman was shaking all over now, and Carrillo waited patiently while he recovered his composure. Finally, he said, almost in a whisper, "How did you find her?"

"To tell you that, Mr. Bowman, would be to tell you details of your sister's life that you should learn, if at all, only from her. And as I have said, I make no guarantees. Use this information, or not, as you wish."

"Is she OK?"

"She does not appear to need rescuing, if that is what you mean. She is safe. More than that I cannot say."

"I don't know what to say. Thank you. I can't believe you would do this for me."

"It was a mere trifle, Mr. Bowman. I had nothing better to do."

"I don't believe. I'm sure you're a busy man."

"I did not say that I had nothing else to do, only that I had nothing better to do."

CHAPTER 30

Hank's Diner was packed with the breakfast rush, but Bowman had a booth all to himself. He had explained that he was expecting company and, given that he was something of a local celebrity, they had accommodated him. He knew most of the patrons, at least by sight. Since his release from the hospital he had become a regular, and the diner, and the town generally, had adopted him as one of their own. People he didn't know would approach him and wish him well. He was not used to that, but he liked it.

His eyes were on the door, so he saw her first, but in a moment or two all eyes were on her, and there was a pause in the noisy bustle of clinking plates and conversation. And she was worth looking at. Clementine Bates wore a sleeveless dress that ended just above her knees, in some kind of floral pattern with lots of green in it, to match her eyes. She wore sandals and carried a small purse. Her dark hair was loose, and just brushed her slender shoulders. Her arms and legs were toned and lightly tanned. She was even prettier than he had remembered.

She spotted him, smiled and started walking towards him as the other patrons returned to their own business and the normal background sounds of the diner resumed. He slid out of the booth and stood to meet her.

"No gun today, Agent Bates?"

"I didn't think I'd need it, Mr. Bowman. Was I wrong?"

Bowman laughed. "No, you won't need it. I'll be good." He felt like he should hold a chair for her, but could only make an elaborate gesture towards her side of the booth. Once she was seated, he slid in on his side.

"Call me Robbie, please. Can I call you Clementine?"

She put her hand on her chin, face scrunched up in apparent serious concentration, and considered for a couple of seconds. "Well — OK. But you're on probation. One slip and it's back to 'Agent Bates.'" Then she smiled again, and her whole face joined in.

"Like I said, I'll be good. Thanks for coming."

"How could I refuse? I don't get many offers of breakfast at Hank's Diner. I hear there's a waiting list for reservations."

"Yes, but I have some pull with the maître d'."

"Apparently."

Just then the waitress arrived to take their orders. Bowman thought she took a proprietorial interest in him and, judging by the look on her face, she was not yet sure that his new friend was suitable. The look said, 'Pretty, for sure, but what else does she have?'

"What'll it be, Sweetheart?" she said to Clementine as she pulled a pencil from behind her ear.

"I'll have a stack of blueberry pancakes, and some coffee."

The waitress arched her eyebrows in surprise and nodded her head in approval. Probably she was expecting a request for yogurt and fruit, or a bran muffin.

"Great choice," Bowman said. "They have six different flavors of syrup to choose from. I recommend the boysenberry."

"It's nice to have options, but I'm a traditional girl. I'll stick with maple syrup, please."

The waitress nodded her approval again, then turned to Bowman. "How about you, Hon'? The usual?"

"Yes, please."

After the waitress had tucked her pencil back behind her ear and retreated, Clementine said, "So how are you? You look good."

Bowman wished he looked better. He was wearing some more of Fernando Flores' clothes, which fit him a little looser now. Presentable, but pretty down-market next to Clementine. And he didn't have all his strength back, or his color. But he felt good.

"I'm fine. No permanent damage. I just need some airing out."

She laughed, a beautiful sound, and her green eyes sparkled. "I guess we could all use airing out from time to time."

They chatted on as if they'd known each other for years. She was so easy to be with, and to talk to, that he wondered why he had agonized so long before calling her.

Their food came. 'The usual' was two eggs over easy, home fries, bacon and toast. And coffee of course.

As she attacked her stack of pancakes, he told her about his past, more than he had ever told anyone before, even some of the raw, sore, sensitive parts. And it felt so right. He didn't feel like he had to hide anything from her or justify himself to her, and she accepted it all without a hint of censure or, which would have been worse, pity.

As he wiped up the egg yolks with his buttered toast, she told him about herself, where she was from, her family, college, her career at the DEA, her running. He was impressed. She sounded like someone who was not easily deterred once she'd set her mind on something.

When they were done eating, she said, "So what now? What are your plans?"

This was it, he thought, the subject that could make or break him. He realized now that a great deal depended on how he handled this, and he struggled to keep his nerves in check and his voice casual and even. He had to choose his words carefully.

"First, I have to go to Oregon. I have a lead on my sister, Bridget, and I need to check it out."

"You definitely should. I hope it works out, for both of you." She paused a moment, then added, "And after that?"

Bowman shifted uneasily in his seat, trying to find the courage to say what he wanted to say.

"After that — well, I could — I mean, if you wanted — but I don't want to put you in an awkward position. I just . . .."

She reached across the table and put a finger on his lips to stop his babbling. Then she reached into her purse and took out one of her cards and a pen. Writing a number on the back of the card, she said, "This is my personal number." Pushing the card across the table to him, she smiled and said, "Try not to lose it this time."

Then she leaned over the table and kissed him lightly on the lips. It tasted of maple syrup.

Before Bowman could react, she slid out of the booth and started walking to the door. He realized then that the entire diner had taken an interest in this little drama, and they were all watching her in silence as she walked to the door.

At the door, she turned back to look at him and said, "Don't take too long, Cowboy, I might get a better offer." Then, with a toss of her head, she stepped through the door and out of the diner.

For a heartbeat there was silence, and then the entire diner erupted in applause.

ABOUT THE AUTHOR

Edwin Markham lives in Austin, Texas. Before moving to Austin and starting his writing career, he practiced corporate law for thirty years, primarily in New York City.

Made in the USA
Columbia, SC
01 April 2020

90308898R00143